FINDING *HOME*

Book 2 of the Mylin Valley Series
By
Angela E. Powell

Let's Connect!

I love hearing from readers! The best way to tell me you've enjoyed my book is to leave a review or rating.

You can find my other books, my blog, or drop me a note on my website: www.angelaepowell.com.

Editing by Doreen Martens
Front cover image by 100Covers

Paperback ISBN: 978-0-9991594-6-0
Publisher Name: Angela E. Powell
Publisher Address:
PO Box 513
Huntsville, Utah 84317
www.angelaepowell.com

Dedication

To my mom. The first person to encourage my writing habit and my lifelong cheerleader.

Chapter 1

Why did she do it? Phillip peered up at the building looming in front of him. In the early dawn, it cast a shadow over the whole parking lot. The rental car purred softly as it idled, and he gripped the steering wheel so tightly the vinyl squeaked, bringing his thoughts back to the present. He didn't want to be here.

Turning the key to the off position and removing it, he climbed out of the little silver Corolla. As he headed toward the hospital entrance, he clicked the lock button twice, then stuffed the keys, and his hands, into his pockets. The car beeped, and he glanced behind him to take a mental note of the location.

He paused before reaching the automatic sliding doors and took a deep breath. *Why did she do it?* He'd been asking himself that question ever since Uncle Richard called yesterday afternoon and told him his mom was in the hospital and he needed to come immediately.

He had packed and headed to the airport last evening, hoping to catch a standby flight, but the first seat available was at five this morning. And though Richard had assured him Mom was stable, he'd been unable to quiet his thoughts during his ninety minutes in the air, out of cell range—convinced that once he landed, there would be a message letting him know she had passed. Then he would have to wonder, forever, why she'd decided to kill herself.

Inside the hospital, he checked his messages for the floor he needed and entered the elevator. He punched the button for the psych ward floor, then stepped back, leaned against the wall, and closed his eyes. *Why? Why? Why?*

The elevator dinged, and he opened his eyes. The doors slid open, and he stepped out.

A telephone rang nearby and continued unanswered. He scanned the hall in each direction looking in vain for a sign and finally headed to a nurses' station to his right.

"Can I help you?" asked the matronly woman behind the desk.

"Uh, yes. They admitted my mother yesterday. Andrea Hawkins. I'm here to see her."

"Do you have the code?"

"Code? Oh, yes." He went through the messages from his uncle again. "One-one-four-four-nine."

The woman nodded and stood up. "You'll need to put any personal items in a locker." She pointed to a bank of small lockers on the wall behind him. "When you're done, I can take you to see her."

He headed toward an open storage box. Placing his phone, wallet, and the rental car keys inside, he double checked his pockets for anything he might have forgotten. Ear buds. He'd wrapped them up and placed them in his back pocket after getting off the plane. Adding them to the pile of his possessions, he tried to block the uninvited image of Mom stealing them to strangle herself from his mind and closed the door. He followed the directions for creating a four-digit pin so he could retrieve his items later, then turned back toward the nurses' station.

The older nurse stood in front of the desk, waiting for him. She offered him a kind smile and motioned for him to follow her. Anxiety twisted in his gut as the woman swiped a badge over an access pad near an imposing double door. Something clicked, and the nurse pushed the door open. He followed her through. The other side looked like a regular hospital hallway. Some rooms stood open, some closed. He glanced into one or two of the open ones. They were empty. At the end of the hall, they entered a gathering space where several patients in gray hospital sweats were sitting. Some watched television, some played card games, and others sat near the windows that overlooked the vast hospital parking lot and stared out. He followed the nurse through the large room into another hallway.

The nurse pointed to an open door. "That's her room. Morning visiting hours end in about twenty minutes."

"Thank you."

The nurse left him and Phillip headed toward the room, hearing voices he recognized. They were arguing. And it was obvious they were both trying to keep quiet.

He paused at the door. Mom sat perched on the edge of the bed, her body angled away from him. She wore the same gray sweats he'd seen the other patients wearing and an ache filled his chest. Richard sat on the edge of a lime green armchair in the far corner, which contrasted with the drab gray and off-white decor. He figured the bright color was meant to add some cheerfulness to the place. Neither had noticed him yet.

"Our mother is fine where she is," Mom said.

Richard shook his head. "I'm not sure that's true, Andi. A nursing home makes sense." His baritone voice cracked slightly as he pleaded with his sister.

Mom slammed her palm on the bed beside her. "No! I told you, this was an accident." She waved her hand around.

Phillip cleared his throat.

"Phillip!" Richard's whole body seemed to relax at the sight of him, and he rose.

Mom glanced at him, but instead of welcoming him, she went silent, turning her back to them.

As Phillip came in, his uncle closed the gap between them, embraced him, then patted him on the back. "Good to see you."

Phillip nodded. Richard's hair and beard were a mix of gray and sliver now, instead of the deep auburn he remembered. His red-rimmed eyes made him look exhausted, but Phillip couldn't tell if it was from crying or lack of sleep. Maybe both.

"Mom?"

Andi stood, turned to face him, and twitched her lips upward. Her hair, too, was no longer the vibrant red he remembered. Since they occasionally talked via video calls, he knew that. But in person she looked much older. The streaks of gray mingled with dull auburn hung limp and tangled on her shoulders. He went over to her and gave her a brief, light hug, which she returned just as lightly. When they parted, she had tears in her eyes. Andi patted his face. "You didn't have to come." She peered around him. "You shouldn't have called him," she said in a slightly harder tone.

"Mom, of course I had to come."

"No, this is all a misunderstanding." She waved her hand at him and sat cross-legged on the bed. "Did your uncle tell you about the misunderstanding?"

Phillip glanced at Richard, who gave a small shake of his head and rolled his eyes upward.

"No."

She made a disgusted noise. "Of course he didn't." She patted the bed beside her, inviting him to sit.

He sat and waited.

"Grandma started taking walks around the neighborhood in the middle of the night. I worked with her doctor and got the problem resolved. But while we were finding ways to help Grandma sleep through the night, I wasn't getting much sleep. I took a couple of sleeping pills before getting Grandma settled but forgot that I'd taken them. I took more before bed. Your uncle showed up the next morning to see how Grandma was doing and found me unconscious." She shrugged. "That's it. It was an accident."

Phillip nodded, unsure what to say.

"And now your uncle is hell-bent on putting Grandma into a nursing home. Which is ridiculous. This was a slight glitch. I can still take care of her." Her voice sounded accusing and a little too high-pitched to be believable.

Someone knocked on the door. All three of them looked that direction. A skinny older man in a white doctor's coat stood in the doorway, holding a pair of glasses in his hand.

"Good morning, Andrea. How are we doing today?"

Mom rolled her eyes, looked away from him, and didn't respond.

Phillip stared at her in surprise. She still sat with her legs crossed, her face screwed up into a pout like a child. He'd never known Mom to be rude to anyone. Her years as a server had given her plenty of opportunities, but she'd always opted for as pleasant an outward demeanor as she could muster. She had carried it over into her daily life. She had plenty of stories about horrible customers, of course, but she'd never allowed them to see her irritation and was never rude.

The doctor sighed and tapped the glasses against his other hand. "I'm Doctor Andrews. You must be her son." He stuck his hand out and Phillip shook it.

"Yes, I am."

"Visiting hours are about to run out for the morning. Andrea, I'll let you bid farewell to your family and maybe we can try to talk after lunch. Richard, your wife called the nurse's desk. I believe they have her on hold for you."

"Thank you," Richard said, and he followed the doctor from the room.

Mom reached over and squeezed Phillip's shoulder. "Go back to California, son. I'm sorry Richard worried you for nothing. Everything will return to normal once they let me out."

Weariness and indecision settled over him. He wanted nothing more than to return to California. He most definitely didn't want to drive to Mylin Valley, where his family all lived. He couldn't leave now. At the very least, he needed to stay until they released her from the hospital. He could at least do that much. But why didn't she want him here?

"It's really not a big deal, Mom. I'd like to stay a few days to make sure you get back into your rhythm."

The corners of her mouth briefly turned upward again. "I am glad to see you," she murmured.

Richard entered again, a concerned expression on his face. "Denise needs some help with Grandma, so I'm going to take off. Come to your mom's house when you're done here, Phillip, and we'll figure out where to get you settled."

"He'll stay with me and Grandma. There's an extra room there."

Richard looked at his sister with raised eyebrows. "You're sure?"

"Of course I'm sure. He's my son."

Richard nodded.

"Is everything okay?" Phillip asked.

"Hmmm? Oh yes, everything's fine." Richard patted his shoulder. "Come to the house when you're done here."

Mom rummaged around in the mostly empty nightstand, which matched the lime green armchair, pulled out a hair tie and put her hair into a loose ponytail.

Richard motioned for Phillip to follow him into the hall.

"I'll be right back, Mom."

She nodded and settled on the bed with a magazine.

"Phil, try to convince Andi to work with the psychologist," Richard said when they were in the hall. He glanced at his watch and rubbed his hand over his beard. "She's refusing to participate in the psychological evaluation. They can only keep her for seventy-two hours, which means they legally have to release her the day after tomorrow, but I'd feel more comfortable knowing they released her because they were confident she's not suicidal, rather than because they have to."

Phillip nodded. "You don't think she's telling the truth about it being an accident, then?"

He glanced at his watch again. "I'm not sure what to think. Andi knew I would stop by yesterday morning, so if she did plan it, she knew Grandma wouldn't be neglected. After the ambulance left, Denise stayed to make sure Grandma was okay and I followed Andi and stayed with her until she woke up. I made sure she knew where she was and what was happening before heading back to the house to help Denise.

"There were some signs Andi was falling behind in Grandma's care. Medications that looked like they'd been skipped or she'd forgotten to give them to Phyllis, a bit of a rash on Grandma's backside as if she hadn't been cleaned properly. Things like that, nothing too severe. Grandma may have dementia, but she still prefers to be independent." He shrugged. "It could go along with her story of not getting enough sleep, but I just don't know. Doctor Andrews thinks Andi has depression and has probably had it for a while."

"Okay. I'll try." Phillip crossed his arms, wondering how on earth he was supposed to get his mother to comply. In the past ten years, they'd talked on the phone frequently, but nothing of actual substance. She would update him on his grandmother's condition, he would update her on his business stuff, and if he were dating anyone, or any funny or interesting stories he had to tell. He wouldn't have considered their relationship to be strained, but somehow being here with his mother in the psych ward made Mom feel like a stranger to him.

"Good boy. I better go so I can help my wife."

Phillip returned to Mom's room. He only had a few minutes to fulfill his uncle's request, but he didn't know what to say, or how to bring it up. He sat on the edge of the bed again and thought about their once-a-week calls they'd kept up since he left home for college. He tried to recall their most recent conversations—her tone of voice, whether anything about their calls had changed—but nothing came to mind.

If she was seriously depressed, wouldn't he have been able to hear it in her voice? At least detect that something was off? He watched Mom as she continued reading her magazine. She wasn't going to allow him to ease into the subject, so he would have to be blunt.

"Mom?"

"Hmm?" She set the magazine on her lap, still open to the page she'd been perusing.

"Why aren't you doing what the doctors are asking you to do?"

"Because I'm not depressed," she said matter-of-factly. "That, and Doc Andrews has been telling your uncle everything. I don't want your uncle knowing all my medical business."

He couldn't help but notice she hadn't yet referred to her brother in any terms that claimed him as her relative. "Well, we can double-check, but I'm pretty sure the psych evaluation has to be kept confidential and only shown to those you allow to see it."

"Apparently not if I don't have a document on file saying who does or doesn't have permission to make medical choices for me if I can't make them myself. Without it, any family who shows up gets to make that decision. Richard has been trying to make plenty of decisions for me since I've been in here."

"Like what?"

"He requested they keep me until I agreed to take that stupid evaluation. Thankfully, they couldn't do that."

"Mom, I'm sure he's just worried about you."

She huffed. "Did you know he's been calling care facilities trying to get Grandma moved into one? Even though I told him I was doing fine taking care of her myself. He wants to keep me imprisoned so he can move her without me fighting back on it. We're supposed to be making these kinds of decisions together, but he's trying to take total control."

A knock sounded on the door, and the matronly nurse he met when he first arrived stood in the doorway. She gave him a sympathetic smile. "Visiting hours are over, I'm afraid."

Phillip nodded. "Can I ask you a quick question before I head out?"

"Of course." The nurse stepped further into the room.

"The psychological evaluation the doctor wants her to take—can that be kept confidential between her and Doctor Andrews?"

"Oh, absolutely. Only those who have your mother's permission to view her records can see the results."

"See, Mom?"

Andi chewed on her bottom lip. "I would rather not take it."

Phillip moved closer to her and picked up her hand. "Mom, please? If you won't do it for Uncle Richard, will you do it for me? It will give me peace of mind before I head back to Cali. You don't have to tell me the results. Knowing you took it, and the doctor is satisfied, is enough for me."

Andi searched his face, and he saw the familiar weariness from years of fighting for what she needed—the lines permanently etched around her eyes and mouth. Maybe that's why he couldn't detect depression in her. Could he have mistaken depression symptoms for the familiar weariness he'd always known her to have?

"Okay. Okay, I'll do it." She squeezed his hand. She looked sharply at the nurse and pointed a finger at her. "I don't give anyone permission to look at it besides me and Andrews. I want that in writing."

The nurse smiled at her. "Very good. I'll let him know and get you the document to sign. We should be able to take care of that first thing tomorrow morning."

"Thanks, Mom."

She nodded. "Now go home and make sure your uncle doesn't move Grandma into a home!"

He gave her a mock salute, adding, "Yes, ma'am," before following the nurse out of the psychiatric ward.

Chapter 2

Back in the rental car, Phillip locked the doors. A habit he had picked up in California shortly after his arrival there. One positive thing about Mylin Valley was the relative safety of the place compared to large cities like the one he'd lived in the past ten years. He leaned his head back against the seat and closed his eyes. With much of his stress and anxiety eased, he was suddenly feeling the lack of sleep that resulted from his attempt at overnight travel. It was a thirty-minute drive from the hospital to Grandma's house. He realized his uncle probably hadn't made it back yet and wondered how his aunt was coping and what issue she was dealing with that required his uncle's help. Richard had seemed pretty concerned after the phone call and looked like he wanted to get on the road as quickly as possible, but he hadn't asked Phillip to come and help.

Although a decade had passed since he left home, he could still picture the roads he needed to traverse to get to Mylin Valley, nestled in the mountains to the east.

Dread settled in his stomach as he traced the roads in his mind. Suddenly, dealing with Mom in the hospital seemed easier than returning to the town he grew up in.

At least he didn't have to go back to the same small, dark apartment. A couple of years ago, Mom had told him that they'd partially torn down the apartment building where they'd rented a basement dwelling when he was a kid and rebuilt it to make townhomes. He wouldn't even have to drive down his old street, since Mom had moved in with Grandma about three years ago to become her full-time caregiver. It would be fine. He backed out of the parking space and headed for the mountains.

About halfway there, his stomach rumbled. He'd eaten nothing since last night, before his flight. He used the car's hands-free system to phone his uncle.

"Phil, is everything okay?"

"Yeah, I'm about to head up the canyon now, but I'm starving. Do you want me to pick up brunch for everyone?"

"Uh, I don't know if your aunt has made anything. I just got to the house. Let me go check with her and call you right back."

"I can wait—" But his uncle had already hung up. Weird. Why did Richard think she had time to make food if she was having a hard time with Grandma? Maybe those red-rimmed eyes of his were exhaustion.

A couple of minutes later, his phone rang. He pressed the phone button on the steering wheel to answer it. "Hey."

"Hi. Brunch would be great. You said you're already in the canyon?"

"I am now, just started up."

"Okay. Do you remember Rosie's Cafe?"

"Yeah, I think so."

"They're the only restaurant up here that's open this early these days. I'll text you our order."

"Sounds good. See you in a few."

A rush of memories flooded into his mind as he traveled the streets of the small town of Mylin Valley, which sat along the bank of the Mylin Reservoir. Summer nights on the beach, cow tipping, taking the school bus down the canyon in high school, and all the horrors that accompanied being stuffed on a bus for an hour with both your friends and enemies. Every memory held the hope of fun times and friends, but ended with a disappointment or pain. Jake getting into a fight, or getting arrested. Getting into trouble himself, coming home to an empty house because Mom worked two full-time jobs. Doing his homework alone. Making dinner for himself.

And while some things had changed—there were more houses where there used to be open fields—much had remained the same. The park in the center of town still had its towering, hundred-year-old evergreens, the soccer field, concession stand, and playground. The two blocks of small commercial buildings were still there. Some appeared to have been updated or had different businesses in them, but overall the area looked the same as it always had.

He parked the car in front of one of the small buildings, which had an old wooden sign above it that read Rosie's Cafe in a sprawling, painted text that was peeling now, and climbed out. Pulling open the old, heavy wooden door, he stepped inside and made his way to the counter, glancing at his phone and reading the text message his uncle had sent.

A group of people stood in line in front of him, so he took a few minutes to look around the old building. He hadn't eaten here very often. They couldn't afford to eat out much in those days. But occasionally the family of a friend invited him to join them. Most of the tables were occupied. Their blue and white gingham tablecloths looked clean and starched, as they had years ago. Wooden crates still lined the walls, stuffed with colorful oversized mugs, knickknacks, and signs with inspirational messages on them.

"Phillip?"

Startled at being recognized, he spun toward the voice, his heart pounding.

A sandy-haired man about his own age and height stood smiling in front of him.

"Scott?"

"Holy crap, dude! It is you!" Scott grabbed him and gave him a bear hug.

Unprepared for such a welcome, he didn't return the greeting.

"How the heck are you?" Scott asked.

"Uh, doing okay. How about you?"

"Great, man! I'm here having an early lunch with the fam." He gestured to the group behind him and invited them to approach. Phillip's stomach flip-flopped at the sight of one figure in the group in particular.

Mr. and Mrs. Fletcher shook his hand, welcomed him, then wandered off to find a table.

"How long are you in town for?" Heather, Scott's younger sister, asked.

Her brown hair was pulled back into a braid, the end of which rested on her left shoulder, and wisps of loose hair framed her face. Her brown eyes were bright and friendly, just as he remembered them. In all his worrying over Mom and stress over returning to Mylin Valley, he hadn't considered he might run into old friends. There were plenty of people he didn't want to see, but the Fletchers had always treated him kindly.

"Um, I'm not sure yet." He hesitated, pulling his gaze away from Heather's face and returning to Scott's. He wasn't sure how much of his family's crisis he should share. Deciding to play it safe, he responded with, "My mom is dealing with some health issues, so I'm here helping her out for a bit."

"Oh, I'm sorry to hear that," Heather said.

"Yeah, man," Scott said, squeezing his arm. "If you guys need anything or you need or want to get out, we can grab some coffee or something while you're here. I'd love to catch up."

Phillip nodded. "I just arrived, so I'm not sure what my days will look like yet, but I'd like that."

"Cool, man. I'll give you my number and you can call me whenever. My days are pretty flexible."

They headed to the counter so Phillip could give his order and Scott could write his number down.

"It's good to see you, Phillip," Heather said, giving him a small wave before joining her parents.

"Thanks. You, too." He felt his face get hot and hoped no one had noticed, especially Scott, who knew how he'd felt about Heather in high school.

Thankfully, Scott was leaning over the counter, scribbling away. "Here you go, dude."

"Thanks."

"Yeah, and seriously, call whenever."

Phillip nodded, and Scott also returned to his family.

He tucked the slip of paper into his pocket and placed his order. He liked Scott; always had. In fact, Scott had been his closest friend growing up. But they'd gotten into a lot of trouble together. He wondered if Scott was still a troublemaker or had straightened up. He regretted not staying in touch, but he'd found it remarkably easy to leave the valley behind and not think about it beyond being the place where his family still lived.

A few minutes later, his food was brought out. He exited the building and climbed back into his rental car. In a few minutes, he'd be at his grandmother's house. The house he'd visited only a handful of times while growing up.

Chapter 3

No one answered the door. He could hear voices, though, so he tested the handle and found it unlocked. Yelling greeted him when he let himself in.

"I'm going to call the police! I swear I am! You get out of my house. You're not supposed to be here!" the high-pitched, frail voice of his grandmother yelled out.

Phillip walked quickly down the short hallway that blocked his view of the living room. It was empty.

"Now, Mother," came Richard's voice. "I swear I'm not lying to you. I am Richard, your son. If you just settle down a bit—"

"No!"

Phillip entered the nearest doorway to the kitchen on his right and saw his petite Grandma Phyllis standing near the stove, stabbing the handle of a straw broom toward his aunt and uncle, who were holding their ground near the kitchen table.

"I know my son. You think I don't know my own son? You aren't him. You aren't!" shrieked the old woman.

"Mom, if you call the police, they'll probably take you to the hospital. You don't want to stay the night in the hospital, do you?" Denise asked. "Let's put the broom down and talk."

Grandma squinted her eyes and made another stab at Denise with the broom. "You think I'm crazy? I'm not crazy.

You two strangers just let yourself into my home. I'll call the police and have you arrested, that's what!"

Phillip cleared his throat. "Can I help?"

"Oh, oh, oh!" cried his grandmother. "A good Samaritan! Please, young man, these two are intruders. Call the police!"

Phillip looked first at his uncle, and then his aunt. Richard looked exhausted and shrugged his shoulders. Denise also looked tired, but less so than his uncle. A thoughtful expression crossed her face.

"Yes, why don't you come in here and help this poor woman, and we'll leave." She motioned for Richard to follow her. As they passed him, Denise whispered, "We'll just step outside for a few minutes and see if her mind resets."

Phillip nodded and stepped further into the kitchen. He put the two bags on the counter and looked at his grandmother. "It looks like they're leaving. I have some food here. Are you hungry?"

She stabbed the broom toward the empty doorway. "Make sure they're gone."

"Okay." He walked back through the doorway. The screen door was closed, but the main door stood open. He could see them sitting on the front porch. He closed the main door in case Grandma came to see for herself, then returned to the kitchen. "All gone."

Grandma visibly relaxed but kept a tight grip on her broom. "What is your name, young man?"

"Phillip Hawkins."

She squinted at him thoughtfully, then shook her head. "How odd. I have a grandson with that name, but he's only ten years old, and you're obviously much older. Must be a sign from the good Lord. I should give you a reward for helping me."

Phillip was stunned for a moment. Grandma remembered him as a ten-year-old? That's how old he'd been when he met her for the first time. Shortly after his tenth birthday party. The party Jake had shown up drunk to and later got arrested on DUI charges. "Oh, that's unnecessary, really. I'm just glad you're okay."

She leaned the broom against the counter and approached him, grabbing both of his hands with her tiny, wrinkled ones. They felt cold and boney. "A brave boy like yourself should be rewarded. Few people would help an old woman nowadays. Now, you stay here and I'll go find my wallet."

He nodded, unsure how else to respond, and decided that if she gave him money, he would return it to her later, or give it to Denise. Grandma left the kitchen through the second doorway, nearest the hallway leading to the bedrooms and the single bathroom. She held onto the walls for support. Turning in a slow circle, he wiped the back of his hand across his forehead and wondered if he should invite Richard and Denise back in or wait a little longer. He unpacked the food while he waited.

After that was done, he listened for his grandmother but heard nothing. He went to check on her and found her sitting in a rocking chair in what he assumed was her bedroom. He realized he'd never seen any part of this house besides the living room and kitchen. Figuring that was a sign it would be okay to let his aunt and uncle in, he returned to the front door to give them an update.

They both let out a sigh of relief and entered the house again.

Denise hugged him. "Sorry you didn't get a better welcome. She's had a rough couple of days without your mom here." She released him, and they returned to the kitchen and brought the food from the counter to the table and sat down.

"How was Andi when you left?" Richard asked.

Phillip shrugged. "She seemed okay. I got her to promise to take part in the evaluation."

Richard sat up straight, his bushy eyebrows raised. "You did! Excellent."

"How did you get her to change her mind?" Denise asked.

"I reminded her about doctor-patient confidentiality. She made it clear she didn't want anyone to see the results except herself and the doctor."

Richard's shoulders sagged. "She won't get the help she needs if she keeps everything hidden away."

"But isn't her trying to hide it a sign that something is, in fact, wrong?" Denise asked.

"I suppose that's true, but it doesn't help us help her," Richard said.

Denise got up from her seat and gave Richard a kiss on the cheek. "I'm sure it will all work out somehow. I'll go see if Phyllis is hungry." She sighed. "Wish me luck!"

Phillip chuckled. "Good luck."

Richard nodded his agreement before picking up his sandwich and taking a large bite.

A moment later, Grandma and Denise returned to the kitchen.

"Mom, I'm glad you're joining us," Richard said, wiping his mouth on a napkin.

Instead of looking suspicious or angry, Grandma now looked a bit bewildered. She stared at Richard, but said nothing, then took her seat at the table.

"Do I know you?" she asked Phillip, her voice low but sweet.

"I'm your grandson, Phillip."

She stared at him wide-eyed. "Oh."

"It's okay if you don't remember me. It's been several years since I was here."

She blinked at him but said nothing more, and he resumed eating.

Denise encouraged Grandma to eat her soup in between bites of her own salad.

"So Phillip, how is life in California?" Richard asked as he finished the last of his meal. "The last time we chatted, you were trying to build some kind of app. Is that right?"

He nodded. "Yeah, I'm still working on that project. Well, kind of. One of our partners backed out about a month ago and the other is considering backing out. The project will be dead in the water if he does, because I can't fund it myself."

"Oh, no! That's too bad," Denise said. "Why are they backing out?"

"One got married last year and his wife pressured him to find a more stable source of income. The three of us met in college and thought it would be cool to partner up, invest in each other's ideas, and help each other until we could gain some recognition and trust with other investors. But we thought we'd have more success by now. Dan, one of my roommates, is the other one who's considering leaving. I think he's tired of trying to come up with ideas to compete in a market that's become pretty tight. Plus, I think he wants to propose to his girlfriend, and I think she's hoping he'll make a change as well."

"What will you do if he leaves?" Richard asked.

Phillip wiped his hands on his napkin and sat back in his seat. "I'm not sure. The app we're making is about seventy-five percent built, so I hope he'll at least stick it out until it's done. We'll both have a little extra cash flow that way. I'm not sure how much, though, and that will impact what I do next."

"What if he quits before the app is done?" Richard asked.

"I'll probably give up on building apps for a while and find a desk job somewhere until I come up with a new idea and convince some investors to go in with me on it."

"Well, I hope for your sake he doesn't back out on you," Denise said.

Richard nodded. "Are you still attending that church you told me about?"

"Yeah, but I haven't gotten very involved," he said, anticipating his uncle's next question. Ever since college, when he'd accepted Christ and told his uncle about it, Richard had urged him to find a good church and get involved, and he had. He liked the people and services, but there weren't many people his age there. He knew nothing about teaching kids, so he stayed away from Sunday school. The men's Bible study group was okay, but they had a tendency to get off topic. The only other group he could join was the singles group, and even though everyone swore it wasn't a matchmaking group, he'd seen enough evidence to the contrary. At the moment, he wasn't looking to date anyone. He needed to get his career on a better footing first.

"Did I have my afternoon vitamins?" Grandma asked.

"Not yet," Denise said. "As soon as you're done with lunch, I'll get them for you."

"I should have them now, so I don't forget."

"I won't let you forget. Besides, you need to eat something first, Phyllis, or your stomach will be upset, remember?"

"Oh? No, I guess I forgot that. Did the phone bill get paid this month? Ed always took care of the bills."

"Yes, Mom," Richard said. "I take care of the phone bill now."

Grandma nodded but seemed lost in thought.

Phillip picked up the remains of his lunch and offered to take everyone else's trash as well. "Which room am I in?" he asked, placing the garbage in the trash can.

"I'll show you," Richard said, getting up from the table.

Phillip followed him out of the room and down the hall. "Grandma and Andi's rooms are at the end. You'll be in my old room." He opened the door and revealed a small room with a twin bed on a log frame and a matching nightstand. There was a closet on the far side, and no dresser.

"This was your room?" Phillip asked.

"Yep, although I had different furniture."

He smiled at his uncle. "Not into the log furniture?"

"Nope. Too bulky for my taste."

"I didn't get any sleep on the flight, so I think I'll grab my stuff from the car and then crash for a while, since Grandma's calmed down."

Richard nodded, and Phillip returned with him to the living room.

"You guys are tired. I can take care of Grandma tonight. Just let me know what to do and when to do it."

Richard looked dubiously at him. "I don't know if we should throw you into the fire so soon, but I'll ask Denise what she thinks. Now, go get some sleep."

He jogged out to the rental, grabbed the small suitcase he'd packed in a rush, and headed back inside. He set the suitcase on the floor at the foot of the bed, deciding to check it later to see if he'd actually brought everything he would need, and lay down on the bed. It was soft, the room warm, the house quiet. And in a few minutes, he was fast asleep.

The house was still quiet when he woke up. The golden hue of the sun shining in his window told him he'd slept several hours. He sat up, stretched, and listened. He could hear the faint sound of a television but nothing else.

He picked up his suitcase, set it on the bed, and unzipped it to reveal his laptop and a tangle of hastily packed clothes. He picked them out one at a time, folded them and set them neatly on the bed. Two shirts, three pairs of pants, one pair of shorts, one pair of PJs, four underwear, no socks, no extra shoes, and his bathroom travel bag.

He sighed and unzipped the travel bag. Thankfully, he had a toothbrush in there. No toothpaste, though. Deodorant, travel shampoo, a razor, but no shaving cream. He would have to make a shopping trip tomorrow, but he could make do for tonight.

Except for socks, what he had would last him for a few days, and he could always wash them if needed. But how long would he need to stay? Other than watching after Grandma tonight, he wasn't sure what his uncle expected of him, or how long to stay. If Mom continued insisting all was well, what reason would he have to stay? And what would determine if he stayed longer or not?

He returned his bathroom items to the bag and the clothes to the suitcase before opening the bedroom door. He took his travel bag across the hall to the bathroom, set it on the counter, then went to find his aunt and uncle.

He found Denise in the kitchen, sweeping the floor. "Did you have a good nap?" she asked.

"Yeah. Everything okay with Grandma?"

Denise nodded. "She's been watching TV in her room. I've done some cleaning, and your uncle has been in the garage going through some old boxes of stuff."

"Did he talk to you about my watching Grandma tonight?"

Denise paused in her sweeping and leaned on the broom. The same broom Grandma had used earlier as a weapon. "Yes. Are you sure? As you saw earlier, she can be a lot of work. And her episodes are unpredictable."

He shrugged. "Yeah, I'm sure. You both look like you could use a night of rest, and I want to be useful while I'm here."

She smiled at him. "All right, then. But if you change your mind, or need help, don't you hesitate to call us. Even if it's in the middle of the night." She pointed her finger at him and tilted her head forward.

"Yes, ma'am." He grinned.

"Let me finish cleaning this floor, then I'll give you the rundown of how to get Grandma to go to bed."

He nodded and returned to the living room. He walked around looking at the photographs lined up on her old piano and wondered if she ever played anymore, or if dementia had taken that away from her, too.

Most of the photos were posed family portraits of his grandparents, his mom, and Richard. One showed Richard receiving his theological degree. He couldn't help but notice there were none of his mother after she turned seventeen. That's when she'd left home to run off with his dad, Jake, and Grandpa Ed had disowned her.

He was surprised to see several pictures of himself, but figured Mom had put them there after she moved in with Grandma.

"All right, Mr. Hawkins. Let me show you what pills Grandma needs to take before bed," Denise said.

He turned and followed her back to the kitchen.

"These are her bedtime pills. Here is what she'll need in the morning, but make sure she eats something first. She doesn't like to eat much, but even a slice of toast will do. In the evening, she often requests a bowl of peaches covered in cream, and there are plenty of both in the fridge."

He nodded.

"She may head to her bedroom around nine o'clock and say she's going to bed, but you'll want to follow her and remind her to use the bathroom and change into her nightgown and adult diaper before she crawls into bed. I've already laid out both. Andi said she usually will put it on if it's laid out, but just check and make sure once she comes out of the bathroom. She doesn't always have an accident overnight, but it happens, and Andi says it's been happening more frequently as of late."

"Got it."

Denise bit her lower lip and looked upward. "Okay," she said after a moment. "I think that's everything. Just make sure she doesn't try to leave the house. She'll get lost."

"Okay. I think I can handle that."

"Great. I'm going to go pull your uncle away from his project so we can get going." She paused in the doorway. "Are you sure you're okay with this?"

"Yep, promise."

She nodded, then turned and disappeared.

He paced the small living room, wishing they would leave so he could be alone to process the last twenty-four hours. A few minutes later, Richard and Denise returned and said their goodbyes. Richard asked him, again, if was sure he didn't want one of them to stay, and he, again, insisted he would be fine. He walked them to the door, gave them both a hug, and blew out a breath as he closed the door behind them. Finally.

Going to Grandma, he asked if she needed anything. She seemed startled by his presence but said she was fine and focused her attention back on her show. He returned to his room and grabbed his Bible, notebook, and pen from the outside pocket of his suitcase before returning to the main part of the house. He plopped these items onto the coffee table, then sat on the couch and rubbed his eyes.

"God, what am I doing here? How am I supposed to help? I'm feeling overwhelmed and incapable of actually being of any help to anyone."

He picked up the notebook and opened it to a blank page, then set it on his lap. "You know how much I don't want to be here. God, I pray for a quick resolution for Mom. I don't know what she needs, or if she's really struggling with depression, but you do. I pray Mom would get the help she needs and not try to hide it. Give me strength to get through this and wisdom to know how long to stay."

It never ceased to amaze him how much his time in the Word brought comfort to him and gave him rest. It had almost become an addiction, something he had to do daily in order to feel normal. He knew Mom had never experienced that same comfort, despite growing up in a Christian home. When he'd told her he'd accepted Christ, an awkwardness had crept in between them, and he could still detect it. "God, Mom needs to know you. She's so resistant. Help her discover the comfort and rest you can bring to her."

Chapter 4

Richard rested his forehead on his intertwined fingers and stared down at his pitiful-looking sermon notes. He had today to finish and review, but he'd hit a brick wall and couldn't focus.

It didn't help that he hadn't slept well last night, again. Every moment, he'd expected a panicked call from Phillip or a call from the hospital telling him Andi had hurt herself. He was too old and too busy to be losing sleep over things he couldn't control. Sitting up straight, he rubbed a hand over his face and beard, smoothing down the frizzy bits he could see in his peripheral vision, shooting out from his face in all directions. He'd never had a situation that bothered him like this week. Why now? Why this?

He picked up the phone receiver on his desk and dialed his nephew's cell number. At least he could put his mind at ease about his mother. Phillip answered on the second ring.

"Hello?"

"Morning, nephew. How did the night go?"

"Good. I got Grandma to bed at nine and she didn't wake up all night. She's up now. I've given her some breakfast and her medication."

"Excellent. Does she know you?"

"No. She was a little on edge at first, but she relaxed after seeing my Bible on the coffee table. She asked me to read her a devotional and pray with her. It's been a good morning."

Richard relaxed into his chair. "That's great. I'm glad things are going well. I'll call the hospital in a bit to see how Andi is, but I wanted to check in with you first. Have you spoken with her this morning?"

"No, I've been pretty busy with Grandma. The evaluation was supposed to be done first thing. I hope she keeps her promise."

"Me too. I guess we'll find out if they release her. If they release her today, I can pick her up. If they don't, you'll need to get her." He didn't want to think what it would mean if they waited until Sunday to release Andi.

"Okay."

"Do you or Grandma need anything?" He picked up a pen and shuffled the papers to locate a blank one.

"No, I think we're good. At some point, I'll need to run to the store for a couple of items I forgot to pack, but I'm not desperate," Phillip said.

"What are they? I believe Denise is running to the store later. I can have her pick them up for you."

"Uh, okay … sure. If it's not too much trouble."

"No trouble at all."

"I need toothpaste, shaving cream, and socks if the store up here has any."

Richard chuckled. "We'll find you some socks. Any brand of shaving cream in particular?"

"Nope, whatever is cheapest will do."

"All right, I'll give this to Denise. I'm working on finishing up my sermon for tomorrow, but call if you need anything."

"Will do. Thanks, Uncle Richard. And remember, don't mention the evaluation or try to find out the results."

"I won't."

Denise entered the room as he placed the phone on the receiver and set a fresh mug of coffee on his desk near his computer.

"Thank you, dear." He rested his elbows on his desk.

"Were you talking to Phillip?"

"Yes. Mom asked him to pray and read a devotional, and everything went well. Oh, and if you're still running to the store later, Phil forgot to pack a few things. I said we'd pick them up. Do you mind?" He handed her the list.

"Not at all. It's sweet that Grandma asked him to read to her." She moved closer to his side and massaged his shoulders. "I still wish you'd found someone else to give the sermon this week."

"I know. Me too. But I checked with everyone who can, and no one was available. At this rate, I don't know how I'll ever retire." He pulled one of her hands to his mouth and kissed it.

"Did you ask any of the small group leaders? I'm still rotating through and visiting each one, and they're doing a great job."

"No, a small group is one thing. The Sunday service is another beast entirely. I don't want them to get discouraged by being thrown into the fire."

"You've mentioned retirement a few times recently. Have you decided that's what you're ready to do?"

He stroked his beard. "Not right away, but soon. Within the next few years, at any rate. I have no idea how to find my replacement, though. We're independent of any larger church organization that could send in a younger pastor. I don't have an associate pastor, and it seems fewer and fewer people are interested in getting involved in the leadership opportunities of ministry."

"Have you talked to God about it?"

He leaned his head back against his office chair. "Not yet."

Denise bit her upper lip and closed one eye. A sure sign she had more to say and was trying to decide whether or not to say it.

He chose not to press his wife for the words she didn't speak. He wasn't ready to admit to her he'd been struggling to hear from the Lord lately. Too many doubts and questions clouded his mind.

"Are you going to tell Phillip about Jake's visit yesterday?" she asked after a moment.

He blew out a breath and picked up the mug of coffee. "I'm not certain." He took a cautious sip of the hot liquid before setting the mug down. "I expect Phil is still pretty angry at his dad. And everything going on with Andi … did you hear Jake say he'd been talking to her for the last year or so?"

Denise nodded.

"What do you think?"

"I think it would be better if he knew. Andi may say nothing, but if she does, it probably won't go over very well. And what if Jake drops by again and Phillip answers the door?"

"He promised he wouldn't."

"Yes, and we all know we can trust Jake to keep his word, right?" Denise asked. "I believe he would handle it better if the news came from you."

Richard nodded. "You're probably right."

Denise leaned over and kissed him. "I'll let you get back to work. Try not to stress about everything. It will all work out."

He waited until Denise closed his office door behind her before picking up the phone and dialing the number for the hospital. Not knowing his sister had been dealing with depression was one thing. Not knowing she'd renewed some kind of relationship with her addicted and abusive ex-husband added a whole different layer to the situation. He wondered if Jake had done or said something that made Andi want to kill herself. Based on their history, it wasn't much of a leap.

"Psychiatric Ward, how may I assist you?"

"Yes, this is Richard Barker. I'm calling to see if my sister Andrea Hawkins has met with the psychiatrist yet and if they'll release her today."

"Do you have the pass code?"

He cleared his throat. "Yes ma'am. One-one-four-four-nine."

"Thank you. One moment and I'll check on that for you."

He drummed his fingers on the desk while he waited. He thought about his nephew. The poor kid only left town to attend college because he was convinced his dad wouldn't bother Andi anymore. Now that Phillip was here, he'd hoped his nephew could find healing for some wounds from his past, but with Jake back in the picture, he wasn't positive the healing Phil needed would happen. The old wounds might just be torn open afresh.

"Mr. Barker?"

"Yes."

"Andrea is with the psychiatrist now. They should be done in a couple of hours. After that, the doctor will write up his report and decide when they'll release Andrea."

"Great. I'll be the one picking her up when she's released. Could you make sure I get the call when she's ready?"

"Sure. It looks like I already have you down as the primary contact, so someone will definitely contact you when she's released."

"Great. Thank you very much."

Hanging up the phone, he read over the paragraph he'd written for his sermon tomorrow, then crumpled the paper and threw it into the trash. Sometimes it was good to hear old sermons again. He flicked his computer mouse and the screen of his PC came to life. He opened his files and scrolled through his past sermons, picking the first one that stood out to him, opened it, and printed it.

Now all he had to do was read through it, make some notes, and he'd be ready to go. "When life gets you down, keep it simple, stupid," he mumbled to himself.

Chapter 5

"Wait, wait. Stay with me until I can return to California."

A car pulled into the driveway, and Phillip walked over to the window above the kitchen sink to see if it was his uncle bringing Mom home from the hospital. It was.

"Dan, come on, man. We talked about this before I left. What changed?"

His college friend and business partner wanted to pull out of their project. He thought he'd convinced Dan to wait until he wasn't dealing with a family crisis so they could talk more.

"Your girlfriend is pressuring you, I know. Didn't you tell her about our agreement to wait until I got back? We're so close."

Mom and Richard both climbed out of the car and headed toward the door. "No, I haven't seen the latest projections. Listen, my mom and uncle just arrived, so I need to go. Please, please don't give up on this until we can discuss it in more detail?"

He paced in the living room, watching the front door. "Thank you. I'll call you back as soon as I can."

They walked through the door as he hung up. Dan had agreed to hold on a little longer, but Phillip would have to find time to work on the app; otherwise, he was certain it would die and he would be job- and probably apartment-hunting when he returned to Cali.

"Hi Mom," he said, approaching her with open arms.

She hesitated, tightly clutching a file folder in her hands, but received his hug. "How is everything here?"

"Good. Grandma has been pretty quiet today, mostly keeping to herself unless she's hungry."

Mom nodded. "Good. I'll go check on her, then take a shower." And she headed to Grandma's room, still clutching the file.

Phillip looked at his uncle, eyebrows raised in a question.

"They said they were confident with the results of her evaluation. The doctor doesn't think she's a harm to herself or others."

"That's good, right?"

"Yeah, it is. Are you still sticking around a few more days?"

Phillip nodded. "I'll stay until Mom is back in her normal routine and doesn't need my help anymore. But my business partner called, and I've got to get more done or he's going to bail."

Richard nodded. "Hopefully, this is the end of the drama." He rubbed his eyes. "Either your aunt or I will drop by a little later to make sure everything is all right."

Phillip felt bad for his uncle; he was obviously exhausted. Him being here might not be much help to Mom, but he hoped that it would give his aunt and uncle enough of a break to catch up on some rest. "You don't have to do that. I'm sure we'll be fine. Besides, you're teaching at church tomorrow. You should go home and rest up."

Richard smiled. "I am pretty tired. But if you need anything—"

"I know. I'll call," Phillip said.

"Oh, I almost forgot. I have a bag for you in the car. Denise picked up those items you needed. I'll grab them."

"I'll walk out with you."

He followed his uncle out to the car in his bare feet and took the bag of toiletries and socks. "Thank you. I really appreciate this."

"No problem. Do you think you'll want to come to church tomorrow?" Richard asked.

Phillip hesitated. "I don't know. I may wait and see how things go with Mom and Grandma." He also wasn't certain he wanted to deal with all the people who might or might not recognize him.

"Everything will be fine," called Mom from the door, startling them both. "I passed that evaluation and everything is great. You go to church with your uncle, if that's what you want. I don't require a babysitter."

Richard raised a hand toward his sister. "Have a good evening, Andi."

"I will. Phillip, I've decided I'm taking a long bath instead. Do you mind fixing some peaches and cream for Grandma?"

"Nope, not at all. I'll be right there."

Mom disappeared into the house.

"Well, I guess maybe I'll see you in the morning, then," Richard said, squeezing his shoulder.

"Yeah." Phillip chuckled and headed into the house.

After getting Grandma her snack, he settled on the couch with his laptop to do some work on the app. Dan mentioned issues with some work flows. If he could get those sorted out and get the project back on track, Dan might follow this through.

He sighed, frustrated that both his friends either had or wanted to back out of this venture for a more stable income than their four, almost five apps were generating. A decision they'd made once their relationships with their significant others had become more serious. Didn't they understand they had to keep working, keep building, project after project? And now they were sidelining him because they wanted to get married.

True, the projects they'd completed were small and didn't bring in a lot of cash. But combined, the four apps they had finished weren't total busts. And the projections for this one had looked fantastic. He remembered Dan's comment about the outlook not looking great anymore and opened his email. He knew they couldn't depend on the statistics, since they were always changing, but this report was pretty grim.

He switched back to programming and worked on it for an hour. Absorbed in his task, he didn't notice when Mom entered the room until she sat in the armchair across from him. He saved his work and shut the laptop.

"Don't let me interrupt. You seem pretty engaged with what you were doing." She had her hair up in a messy bun and wore a matching green pajama set.

"No, it's okay. Glad to be home?"

She rolled her eyes. "You have no idea."

He leaned forward, resting his elbows on his knees. "Mom, out of curiosity, what would it take for you to consider putting Grandma in a care facility?"

Andi gave him an annoyed look. "Nothing. I would never consider it. I want to care for her here, in her own home, until she takes her last breath." She set her mouth in a determined line.

He thought about the previous day, when his grandmother demanded that he call the police. "Does she ever …" What was the word? "Get combative with you?"

She narrowed her eyes. "No, why? Did something happen?"

He told her about the previous day.

Mom shook her head. "That is why I don't want to put her in a facility. She wouldn't know anyone. I've been caring for her for so long that even on the days she doesn't remember who I am, she's still comfortable with me. Like, somewhere in her brain, she knows I'm safe. She wouldn't have that in a facility where she has multiple nurses and doctors and strangers all the time. I can't do that to her." Mom was getting agitated.

"Okay, okay," he said reassuringly. "I'm just trying to understand the situation better and realizing how long I've been gone." He looked down at the floor. "I should have come home more often. I *should* come home more often," he said, looking up at her.

"Oh, Phillip." She stood and moved to sit next to him on the couch. "You left to attend school and start living on your own." She ran her fingers through his hair. "That's how it's supposed to work." She dropped her hand to her lap, and he straightened, turning his head to look at her.

"Yeah, but most kids at least visit for holidays; I haven't even done that. I never meant to leave you alone, Mom. I always meant to come back and take care of you, or find a nice little place near the beach and move you closer to me. But I haven't been able to do that yet." He realized his business partners might view their situation this way with their significant others, but their wives and girlfriends had limits to how long they would wait. He didn't have a timetable for making sure he took care of Mom's needs. Guilt stabbed at him. He should work harder. Do more to make that happen. She'd spent his entire childhood busting her butt so he would have enough to eat. He could put more effort into his career to keep her comfortable.

Mom closed her eyes and smiled. "Mmm, going to the beach every day, even in the winter. That sounds nice." She opened her eyes. "But I have a job to do here. Grandma needs me. I won't lie, though. Having you around for holidays would be nice."

He debated whether he should push her further and ask about the signs of neglect his uncle had mentioned, but decided against it. Now that she was home, he could observe for himself how well Mom cared for Grandma. Once he had his proof, he could bring it up.

She patted his leg. "Well, I need to take care of some things, and return some phone calls. I'll be in my room if you or Grandma need me."

He nodded as she stood and stared thoughtfully after her as she headed down the hallway.

Chapter 6

Phillip stood outside Mylin Valley Life Church and stared up at the yellowing sign on the front of the brown brick building, his hands in his jean pockets. The faint sounds of the worship team practicing inside reached his ears. He hadn't been here for a service since he was eleven.

Jake had recently been released from jail and managed to keep a job for more than a few months. Mom was finally able to quit working one of her two jobs. Until then, Richard and Denise had watched him after school and occasionally on the weekends, since no one could rely on Jake. He'd begged Mom to let him join the after-school basketball team and convinced her he was old enough to not need a babysitter anymore.

He walked up to the doors of the church. It was probably easy for Mom to agree. She never liked it when he had to go to church with his aunt and uncle.

The only thing he'd missed was hanging out with Scott, but he'd hung out with Scott nearly every other day of the week, so it hadn't been that big of a deal. He pulled the door open and realized it might surprise people to see him there of his own accord. He wondered if Richard had ever mentioned to his congregation the fact that he'd accepted Christ. He couldn't imagine his uncle thinking that would be necessary. But pastors used family as an example all the time.

He paused in the foyer, half expecting everyone to stop and stare at him. In a small town like Mylin Valley, people always knew facts about you, but you could never be certain who knew what, or when they would approach you and ask you about whatever they'd heard.

"Hey, man! I am stoked you came today," Scott said, slapping him on the back. "How's your mom?"

"Thanks. She's doing okay." This morning, Mom had gotten up before him and had helped Grandma bathe. He'd checked Grandma's medicine containers and found them all full again, so Mom had apparently refilled them. With her preoccupied, he made breakfast, but while Mom seemed cheerful enough, she ate little and insisted he go to church, which wasn't like her.

Something about her cheerfulness made him uneasy, though, like she was trying too hard to appear happy. He tried to put those thoughts from his mind. Time would tell. "Hey, I'm available to grab coffee this week if you still want to."

"Definitely. Let's do it, let's make a plan," Scott said.

"How about tomorrow morning?" Phillip asked. "Is the Old Place still around?"

"Yeah, it is, and tomorrow works perfecto. Wanna say nine-ish?"

"Works for me."

"Excellent."

The Old Place was the coffee shop near the fire station. It was one of the oldest buildings in Mylin Valley and had originally been a town meeting house. He and his high school buddies had spent a lot of time there. It was one of the few places he had actually missed when he left.

"Scott, do you have Mom's phone?" Heather asked, walking up to them. "Hi Phillip."

He smiled and nodded in greeting. She wore her hair down today. And the dark blue jeans, worn brown boots, and teal V-neck blouse with short, flared sleeves revealed a more feminine side of Heather than her usual cowgirl getup did. And he liked it. A lot. He couldn't help but wonder if either of them had noticed he was wearing the same t-shirt he'd worn the day he arrived, when he'd run into them at the cafe.

"No, why would I have it?"

Heather shrugged. "She's looking for it and thought she gave it to you."

Scott patted all his pockets, then shook his head. "Nope. I had it for a minute to look something up, but gave it back to her."

"Okay. How's your mom doing, Phillip?"

He cleared his throat. "She's good."

"Great. I was about to go save seats. Do you want to sit with us this morning?"

The thought of sitting next to Heather made the room feel suddenly warm. But he wasn't about to pass on the opportunity. "Sure."

She smiled. "Great, I'll save you a spot too, then." She turned and headed into the sanctuary.

He returned his attention to Scott, who had a slight smirk on his face, which Phillip ignored. They hadn't become reacquainted enough to discuss his sister. "I'm going to go find my aunt and say hello. I'll find you inside."

He didn't get very far before a short, white-haired woman accosted him. She grabbed his arm as he passed her and squeezed it. "Phillip Hawkins?"

He stopped, and his heartbeat quickened at the firm, icy grip. He didn't have to hear the woman's voice or see her face to know who stopped him. Mrs. Diana Eberly. "Yes, ma'am," he said, turning to face her.

She looked him over, a frown on her stern features. "I heard you were in town, but I didn't expect to see you here."

As ever, words escaped him in the presence of this old woman. She'd appeared ancient to him as a boy but didn't seem to have aged at all since his childhood.

"How's your mother? She spent a couple of nights in the hospital, correct?"

"Yes ma'am, she did. But she's home now and doing well."

Mrs. Eberly narrowed her eyes at him, then gave a curt nod. "I'm glad you're here to take care of her. That is a child's duty to their parents when they get older. You seem to have grown up well, young man. Of course, I always thought you looked like a good, well-behaved boy, and that wasn't exactly the case, was it?" She released her grip on his arm.

He shifted his weight from one foot to the other. "I guess I did get in a bit of trouble when I was younger."

"Humph. Considering who your father is, your youthful indiscretions didn't surprise anyone. I suppose only time will tell if you outgrew them or not." And she walked off.

Phillip blew out a breath and shook his head. Mrs. Eberly, the town watchdog, and gossip. She'd caught him and Scott several times sneaking around town after dark. Even if all they'd done was shoot hoops at the park, she would call the sheriff, or their parents, and give them an earful. He couldn't believe the old bat was still alive.

He walked around the church, peeking through the open doors, noting the rooms that had changed and the ones that hadn't, until he found his aunt. She was sitting alone in the prayer room. He knocked lightly on the door and stepped in.

She glanced up from the book she was reading, then closed it and got up from her seat. "You came. That must mean Andi is doing well?"

He shrugged. "I suppose."

They hugged. "What does that mean?"

"It seems she's trying too hard."

"Trying too hard to what?"

"I'm not sure. Be cheerful? I feel like she wants me to see that she's taking extra good care of Grandma. Maybe I'm reading too much into it. She only got home yesterday. But it's weird."

Denise sighed. "I think we'll have to wait a few days. Let things settle. Have you considered how long you will stay?"

He shook his head. "I'm playing it by ear right now, but some work stuff has come up that I need to take care of. I should be able to do it remotely, though."

She nodded. "Well, keep us updated, and if you need anything, let us know."

"I will. I better go find my seat. Talk to you later."

Chapter 7

"Good morning." Richard shook hands with several people who had entered the sanctuary at the same time. "How are you all doing today?"

He received several nods and, "Good, thanks. Yourself, Pastor?"

To which he responded with his usual "Doing well" or "Can't complain," before they moved on.

"Pastor?" A woman in her mid-forties approached him.

"Yes, ma'am."

"I was wondering if I could ask you to pray for my daughter? She's having a hard time at school but isn't willing to open up and speak to me about it. I'm at my wits' end and don't know what else to do." Tears formed in the woman's eyes.

"Of course. Let's step out of the aisle a bit here and we'll pray." They took a few steps away from the main sanctuary door, and Richard prayed for wisdom and patience for the mother to know how best to communicate with her daughter so she would open up about what was happening at the school. He also prayed God would work in the situation at school, whatever it was.

Two other people waited nearby until he finished praying. He smiled at them and they came closer.

"Pastor, we're short some staff in kids' church and our backups aren't available, either," Ann, the head of the children's department, said. "We could ask parents to help, or have the kids be part of the service today. What would you prefer?"

He looked at the woman he'd placed in charge of Sunday school and wondered why she never took charge of what he'd entrusted her with but always came to him looking for help. Had he made her believe that's what she had to do, or was it something else? "What would *you* prefer?" he asked.

"Oh, uh, well, I think asking parents is a good idea."

He nodded. "Okay. I agree."

She beamed and headed off to the classrooms.

"It's about the temperature in this building, Pastor," an older gentleman said. "It's too dang cold in here."

Richard sighed. "I'll see what I can do."

The man walked off, and Richard ran his hand over his beard.

"Good morning, Pastor."

"Morning, Mrs. Eberly. How are you today?"

"Doing well. It's nice to see Phillip here. I'm glad he came home to help his mother. You look tired, so I can imagine you're glad he's here to help as well."

He nodded. "It's good to have him home again. How is your Bible study doing?"

Four years ago, Mrs. Eberly had left his church after he'd made some changes in the way he conducted his service, trying to make it more of a hands-on experience for his members rather than a lecture. She'd taken several of the older women and started a Bible study in her home that was structured after a more traditional church setting. But many of the women had returned after hearing good things about the changes he'd made. In the last couple of years, Mrs. Eberly herself and returned, but she still held her little Bible study.

"It's going well, thank you. You know I volunteer at the Catholic church food bank once a month. They are holding a food drive in two weeks. You should make an announcement about it."

He nodded. "I will do that." He checked the time. "I'm heading to my office to pray before worship begins."

Mrs. Eberly nodded, and he left her, hurrying along the side of the sanctuary, hoping to avoid any more questions, complaints or prayer requests, and made his way to his office, where he closed the door and sat behind his desk.

His sermon notes sat on the desk and he glanced through them, and added a couple of notes at the top about announcements he needed to make that morning. Then he sat back in his chair and closed his eyes.

Once again, he found it difficult to find the words to pray. All that came to mind was questions. He was supposed to shepherd these people; lead them to Jesus. But had he succeeded?

Denise led a prayer group every week teaching prayer, yet very few came. Still, they asked him or Denise to pray for their needs. He didn't mind praying for his church members, but when you had hundreds of prayer requests every week, it was hard to keep up. Didn't they realize he didn't have time to sit around and pray for their needs all day long? They needed to know how to pray for themselves, to have their own relationship with Jesus, develop their own communication with Him. That had been his message for the past twenty-plus years.

He let out a deep sigh. He knew many of the members of the church prayed for their own needs. They simply felt better knowing the pastor was also praying. "Where two or more come together to pray ..." he mumbled to himself.

But his leaders, the ones he had carefully selected to help him, still approached him to make final decisions on small things. He'd tried to set up his church the way that Moses, in the Old Testament, had organized leadership. He was supposed to deal with the toughest cases, but his leaders were supposed to know their roles and stand in them with authority. So why didn't they? Why did everyone continue to look to him as the end-all, be-all to every question, complaint, or request?

He'd been the pastor here for over twenty years. What did he have to show for it? If he retired, he had no replacement. No one to carry on his legacy. And what was his legacy? A church full of people who couldn't stand on their own faith; who complained about the most ridiculous things? The band was too loud, or not loud enough. The building was too cold or too hot. The carpet in the Sunday school rooms wasn't soft enough for the kids.

He opened his eyes and sat up straight. "God, what have I accomplished here? I rejected the old traditional ways of doing church because I didn't want to control people through rules and traditions. And I still have a church full of people who act like I'm one of those pastors. What have I done wrong?"

He buried his face in his hands and sat in the enveloping silence of his office, hoping, but not expecting, a straightforward answer to his pleading questions.

A knock sounded on the door.

"Come in."

An usher stuck his head in the door. "Pastor, there is a woman here who wants to join a small group, but there isn't one on a day she can attend. She wants to know what the process is for getting a new group started."

He ran a hand over his face and beard. Case in point, his ushers should know the answer to this question. "There should be some fliers in the main office about that. But have her find me after church if she still has questions."

The man nodded and left.

The band started playing, and he knew it was time to go back into the sanctuary. For the first time in his position as pastor, he didn't want to. He realized he would put on a show today. Exhaustion had seeped into his soul and his body, and he had nothing left to give to his people. "God, give me strength," he whispered.

Chapter 8

The chairs were arranged in circles, and nobody seemed to find this odd besides himself. Each circle contained six or seven chairs, and there were no defined aisles. The sanctuary looked as though it had been set up for a luncheon but they forgot the tables.

He wove his way through the maze of chairs and people until he reached the spot near the front where Scott and Heather were. "This is different."

"Yeah, I guess it is," Scott said. "We've done service this way for, what, three years now?" He looked at Heather, who nodded. "So it's pretty normal for us now."

Richard had told him about changes he'd made, but he hadn't realized to what degree. "What is the purpose of the circles?"

"Pastor Barker doesn't give traditional lecture sermons anymore," Heather said. "He presents a passage in the Bible, teaches on it, then encourages us to discuss the passage with each other in smaller groups. Usually there are questions up on the screen for us to consider and talk about. After a while, he'll lead a larger discussion, where we go through the questions together and hear how other groups answered those questions."

"Sounds interesting."

"It is. We really like it," Scott said.

"Doesn't it make it a little awkward during worship?"

Scott shook his head. "Everyone feels free to wander, or kneel, or whatever. You'll see."

Just then, the band walked up on stage to begin the service. Phillip put his Bible and notebook on a seat and looked around as families entered the sanctuary. He noticed Scott's parents sitting with Mrs. Eberly, who appeared, as he always remembered her, somewhat irritated. An older couple joined their circle, setting their things on two seats directly across from where he stood. He nodded at them in greeting. They smiled at him before moving out of the circle to face the front and read the words to the songs on the screen.

Bodies spread out across the large room as the worship leader began singing. Many swayed with the music. Some had their eyes closed and hands raised; some knelt on the ground. Still others sat in chairs, praying, reading, or simply watching. A few individuals had found enough space in the back to dance.

It was nothing like he remembered his uncle's church being when he was a kid. The atmosphere was relaxed, not stuffy and formal. Even the older ladies who still dressed up in their Sunday best looked at ease, clumped together near the middle. They didn't sway or raise their hands above their shoulders, but they weren't scowling at anyone who showed a little more passion for their worship, either.

He glanced at Scott, who stood between their circle and the next with one arm stretched in the air, his eyes shut tight. Heather stood directly in front of him in the middle of the circle. She held her hands in front of her torso, although he couldn't tell if she had them clasped or folded, but her head was slightly bent as though she were praying. He stared at the back of her head and wondered if she was thinking about him. The way he was thinking of her at that moment. Her opinion of him shouldn't matter. He knew she probably hadn't thought much about him in the past ten years. He hadn't thought about her. At least not for a long time. But the feelings he'd had in high school all came rushing back each time he saw her.

He tried to focus on worship, but this song wasn't familiar to him and his eyes refused to stay on the screen where he wanted them, drifting back to Heather instead. So he closed them.

The worshipful singing ended, and Richard took his place behind the lectern. A hum of conversation and shuffling filled the sanctuary as people made their way to their chairs. Phillip took his seat, while Heather took hers to his left and Scott on his right. The elderly couple returned and took their seats across the circle from them, and a teenager with unnaturally bright red hair slid in and slouched into a chair, crossed his arms and stared at the floor.

"Today I want to talk about attunement," Richard said. "Or rather, our need to feel seen, heard, and understood. Let's turn to John 4 and we'll start in verse 7."

Phillip had to turn his head slightly to see his uncle on the stage. Scott's head partially blocked his view, but that didn't stop him from noticing how tired Richard looked. When he first arrived, he'd assumed the situation with Mom was the reason for Richard's exhausted appearance. But he'd been here three days now and still his uncle didn't look any more rested. Could Richard be dealing with his own health issues and not telling him?

"Verse seven tells us, 'When a Samaritan woman came to draw water, Jesus said to her, "will you give me a drink?" His disciples had gone into the town to buy food. The Samaritan woman said to him, "You are a Jew and I am a Samaritan woman. How can you ask me for a drink?" for Jews do not associate with Samaritans.'

"Take a moment and consider this situation. This woman comes to draw water, like she does every day, and she sees a Jewish man sitting there. She doesn't expect any conversation because the Jews don't associate with 'her kind.' But then he asks her for a drink. Her first response is, 'Uh, you know I'm a Samaritan, right?' She's probably looking around, wondering if she's being set up. Maybe this Jewish man is playing a trick on her. Because Jewish people never seek to see, hear, or understand Samaritans. It doesn't happen.

"Jesus responds in verse ten and says, 'If you knew the gift of God and who it is that asks you for a drink, you would have asked him and he would have given you living water.'

"Obviously, he's speaking of the sacrifice he's going to make by giving his life for the sins of the world, hers included. But he's also telling her he doesn't care if she's a Samaritan. He knows what she needs and what she's looking for.

"She doesn't pick up on this, though, and instead quizzes him about the living water, as if it's a tangible thing in our physical realm. Eventually Jesus asks her to get her husband, and she responds she has no husband. In verses 17 and 18, Jesus calls out her sin of living with a man who is not her husband, and she is amazed. Not repentant, mind you. She calls Jesus a prophet and changes the subject. Why? She might have been uncomfortable. She might have thought Jesus was going to scold her for breaking the law. Maybe she'd been thinking about this question for a long time and recognized this was her first and possibly only opportunity to get it answered.

"Whatever the reason, Jesus uses her question to reveal himself to her as the Messiah and tells her in verse 23, 'Yet a time is coming, and has now come when the true worshipers will worship the Father in Spirit and in truth, for they are the kind of worshipers the Father seeks.'

"And it's clear by her next statement that she doesn't understand what this Jewish man is telling her, because she says, 'I know Messiah is coming. When he comes, he will explain everything to us.'

"Now, skip down to verse 39. The Samaritans from that town believed in Him because of the woman. They believed he was the Messiah, so when the Samaritans came to him, they urged him to stay with them, and he stayed for two days. And because of his words, many more became believers.

"It astonished the disciples that Jesus was speaking to a Samaritan woman. It took them a while to accept that Jesus' message was meant for more than the Jews. Even after Jesus returned to Heaven, they only preached to the Jews until they finally got God's message that it was for the entire world. Not only for those who followed the law of Moses and were chosen to be God's holy people.

"In your groups, I want you to discuss this passage of scripture. Think about individuals in our community who we might not want to invite to church. Ask yourself why not. Talk about experiences you've had being left out, how it made you feel, how it might have been different if you'd been included instead.

"We all crave being seen, heard, and understood. But sometimes we choose not to see, hear, and understand people. Why is that? What can we do to be more like Jesus was with the Samaritan woman when it comes to those in our community?"

Richard left his position at the lectern and sat in a chair on the stage, taking a swig of water from a bottle that had been placed underneath it. The questions he'd asked them to consider and discuss, along with the Bible verses he'd referenced, appeared on the two large screens on either side of the stage.

Phillip read them again, then glanced at Richard, who had leaned back in his chair and stared at the ceiling.

"Okay, we should tackle the first question. Anyone have any insight?" Heather asked.

"Well, many of the kids I mentor hate the idea of religion," Scott said. "It's not so much that I wouldn't want to invite them, but I've had conversations with them about Christianity and they've told me they wouldn't be comfortable in a church, no matter the religion."

"Have they said why?" the older woman asked.

Scott nodded. "They don't feel they'd be accepted or welcomed with their piercings, hairstyles, and lifestyle habits."

"What about you, Jonah?" Heather asked the lone teenager in the group. "Would your friends feel that way?"

The boy remained slouched in his seat, arms folded. He shrugged his shoulders.

Phillip saw a look pass between Heather and Scott. Scott moved so that he was sitting next to the boy and whispered to him.

"Anyone else have an example for that first question? Who in our community might we think twice about inviting to church and why?"

Phillip thought about Mom. Her experience with church had been negative. She saw it as a bad thing. "Thinking about this question from my mom's perspective, I wouldn't consider inviting her because she's so angry about her experience with it. She wouldn't be comfortable, and wouldn't be in a frame of mind to receive anything if she did."

Heather regarded him thoughtfully and nodded before glancing around the circle to determine if anyone else wanted to contribute. No one did.

Scott was still talking quietly with Jonah, but it looked as though the boy was thawing from his bad mood.

"Well, I guess we're ready for the next question," Heather said, looking up at the screen.

Phillip kept his eyes on her. He didn't remember her being this outgoing and taking the lead, though she'd always had a quiet confidence. Though she talked little, no one ever thought she was shy, because when she did express herself, it was always so matter-of-fact. She was unapologetic about her opinions but refused to offer them unless specifically asked.

"What experiences have you had being excluded from a situation? How might things have been different if you'd been included?" Heather read from the screen.

He remembered all the times he'd attended church with his aunt and uncle. He'd been an outsider because he attended irregularly. How would life have been different? He wasn't sure. Would he have accepted Christ sooner? But he'd answered the last question. Someone else could answer this one.

"Um, I don't have a lot of experiences being left out," Heather started. "But I remember there was a time in high school when the popular girls would tease me because I didn't dress the way they did, or do my hair and makeup unless I had a competition that required it. And in that case, my makeup was always way over the top. For a while I felt I wasn't as pretty as they were, and that was uncomfortable."

Phillip stared at the floor, trying to hide his grin. He couldn't imagine her not feeling pretty, and he certainly couldn't ever remember a time when he hadn't found her so.

"If they hadn't made fun of me ..." Heather paused, considering. She shrugged. "I guess it's possible we could have become friends, but I didn't trust them to accept me for who I was. I might have had the opportunity to invite them to church if things had been different. I don't know." She looked around the room, and when her gaze reached Phillip, she gave him a small smile.

"I've been left out of tons of things," Jonah piped up.

"Would you like to share one?" Scott asked.

Jonah shrugged. "My parents won't let me do hardly anything with my friends because they're worried my friends will be a bad influence on me. If they wouldn't do that, then I could show them they can trust me."

"Well, perhaps there's a reason they believe that?" the older man, who had said nothing until now, asked. "I know my friends were always trying to get me to go astray as a youngster."

Jonah glared at the man. "They don't even know them."

"That is a tough situation, Jonah," Heather said. "Because you're wanting some independence, but it sounds like your parents aren't quite ready to let you have it."

"Yeah. But I have to listen to them until I'm eighteen."

Scott rubbed the kid's shoulder. "I am pretty sure I know the answer to this already, but humor me. Have you talked to your parents about it?"

Jonah rolled his eyes. "Yeah, they don't listen and we just argue."

"If you want to talk more after service, I might have some ideas on how to change that. Only if you're interested. I don't want to stick myself into your business if you don't want me there," Scott said.

Jonah shrugged. "Sure, whatever."

"Okay, last question," Heather said. "Even though we all desire to be seen, heard, and understood, sometimes we choose not to see, hear, and understand others. Why is this, and how can we be more like Jesus was with the woman at the well?"

He was trying to understand what was going on at home, but it sure seemed like Mom didn't want anyone to recognize or understand what was going on with her. But that wasn't what the question was asking, and he didn't need to share his family business with a group of mostly strangers.

"That's a hard question to answer," the older woman said. "There are so many variables. I mean, I don't really wish to spend time with someone who is on drugs all the time. I wouldn't feel safe with that person. But those people still need Jesus, too. So someone needs to reach out to them."

"That's a great point," Scott said. "This is a hard question to answer."

They discussed the nuances of the question in more detail, but none of them came up with any great examples or solutions.

After a while, Richard got everyone's attention back on him and went through each question, inviting every group to offer any answers they may have come up with.

"Hey, is Pastor Barker doing okay?" Heather leaned over and whispered to Phillip.

He shrugged. "As far as I know. He and Denise have been helping Mom with my grandma while she's dealing with her health issues, and I think that has him tired more than usual. Why do you ask?"

She glanced at the stage where his uncle stood and frowned. "Usually he walks around the room and speaks with each circle, but today he just sat on stage. He does look tired, though, so maybe that's all it is."

Her concern for Richard touched him, but also created more guilt. He should know what normal behavior for his uncle was. Despite talking to them frequently, he'd lost touch with his family. There were too many things that couldn't be conveyed over the phone. He wondered if anyone else had noticed this off behavior from Richard and decided he would find time to talk to his uncle about it.

After the service, Scott disappeared with Jonah.

"So, what did you think of our unusual service?" Heather asked.

"I like it. It really makes you think about the message."

"I agree. I'm glad you came today."

"Thanks. I should probably head out and check on things at home."

Chapter 9

The Old Place, actually called Old Town Coffee, was a small, nondescript brick building that had been well maintained since its erection in 1860. A plaque near the entrance told its history. Inside, the place was decorated in the fashion of an old soda shop, with vintage-looking tables, chairs, and booths.

Phillip stood in line scanning the chalkboard menu that hung above the checkout counter. He remembered the menu being a lot smaller when he was in high school, offering only basic hot coffee drinks and a few pastries. Now they had fancy hot and iced coffee drinks, juices, teas, and even ice cream.

When he reached the counter, he ordered a drip coffee with a little cream and one packet of sugar. Once he received his order, he joined Scott at a booth and sat across from him, setting his cell phone face side down on the table.

"So what's up, man? What have you been up to in the last decade?" Scott asked.

Phillip shrugged. "I have a degree in business and minored in computer programming, and I'm working to create a new startup building apps. That has been hit or miss, though, so I sometimes design websites for people and businesses to make ends meet."

"Nice."

"So, what about you?"

"Well, I was competing in every outdoor sport I could find until about four years ago. Skiing, mountain biking, dirt bike racing, swimming—you name it, and I probably competed in it."

"I can't say I'm surprised, but why did you stop?" Phillip asked.

Scott sighed. "I started falling behind. Couldn't keep up with people younger than me anymore, and it really messed with me. I used performance drugs to stay in the game. Thankfully, that didn't last long. I got myself clean and decided to teach kids the sports I love instead. And I've started helping Heather a little on her horse rescue."

"She actually created that horse rescue she was always talking about?"

Scott grinned. "Yeah, but her goals for the place have shifted in the last few years."

"Oh yeah? How so?"

"Heather recently got her bachelor's degree in psychology, with a minor in neuroscience. Right now she's applying to get into the master's program. She wants to use some of her rescue horses to start a therapy ranch. She already has a few students because she's convinced a few, already licensed therapists to work on the ranch and mentor her."

"Wow. That's incred—"

"I know you, don't I?" Two manicured hands with red-painted fingernails rested on their table.

Phillip glanced at the face that stared at him. His stomach dropped. The woman's long, perfectly curled blond hair was tied loosely in a ponytail and hung over her shoulder. She wore a light gray, low-cut summer dress with matching cowboy boots. She did indeed know him. And Scott, too, but she wasn't looking at Scott. He didn't respond.

Her bright red lips pursed, and she pointed a finger at him. "We dated, didn't we?"

He cleared his throat. "Hi, Casey."

She grinned and clapped her hands, then slid into the booth next to him. Phillip moved over and rolled his eyes at Scott, who hid the lower half of his face behind his mug, which wasn't big enough to hide his amusement.

Casey linked her arm with Phillip's. "Forgive me. I can't, for the life of me, remember your name." She looked at Scott and squinted. "I know you, too. You're … one of the Fletcher boys."

Scott set his mug down. "Yep, but which one?" he asked, a mischievous glint in his eyes.

She waved a dismissive hand toward him. "Oh, I don't know. It's been forever since I've been in this tiny town, and I'm not very good at remembering names. Remind me? Please?" she asked, transforming her face into a pout.

Scott raised his hand like he was answering to roll call in school. "Scott."

"Phillip," he said, leaning away from her and reclaiming his arm.

"Right. We dated the summer after junior year."
Phillip nodded.

"So, what have you boys been up to since high school?"

Phillip and Scott looked at each other. "Not much. How long are you and your family here this time?" Scott asked.

Casey's father, Calvin Calloway, owned a good chunk of property in Mylin Valley, which they leased, mostly to local business owners. They were the wealthiest family in Mylin Valley. At least when they were here. They owned a mansion on the opposite side of the lake, where they resided about a quarter of the year. Growing up, Phillip remembered seeing Casey around town every summer. Occasionally, her younger sister Caitlin was with her, but mostly it was just Casey. During their high school years, she flirted with all the boys, dated whoever she wanted, and dropped them when she lost interest. And Phillip had been one of them.

"It's just me visiting this time." She sighed dramatically. "I needed a break from city life. But you didn't answer my question. I want to know what's been happening around here. What's the latest news from this neck of the woods?" She folded her arms on the table and looked at each of them.

"Same old, same old," Scott said. "Not much changes around here."

Casey rolled her eyes. "You're no fun. How about you, Phillip? Do you have any local gossip for me?" she said, turning toward him and running a hand lightly down his arm.

Phillip shook his head. "I'm only here for a visit, too. Only arrived a few days ago."

Casey gasped in mock astonishment. "You escaped this sleepy little town? How very Sweet Home Alabama of you. Where do you call home now?"

"California."

"Oh, I adore California. At least parts of it. Which part are you in?"

Phillip sighed, wishing he could figure out how to make Casey go away. He glanced at Scott, who was enjoying the show. "Thousand Oaks area."

"Near wine country. I love wine country. How did you end up there?"

"I got my business degree there." Phillip took a sip of his coffee.

"Business degree. Impressive," she said.

Phillip picked up his phone and checked the time. "I have to go pretty soon. I have some stuff to take care of today."

"Well, I won't keep you," Casey said, getting up. "But we should catch up some more while you're here." She winked at him and handed him a business card with her information on it.

Phillip took the card and said nothing.

"In fact, I'm hosting a party at the house tonight. You should both come."

"Maybe," Scott said.

"We'll think about it," Phillip said.

"Great! It starts at seven. See you later," she said, wiggling her fingers at him and turned to go.

Scott chuckled. "Well, that was fun."

Phillip shook his head, then glanced around the side of the booth to make sure Casey was actually gone.

"Would you ever date someone like her again?" Scott asked.

"No. Oh no. No, no, no," Phillip said. "Never."

"Are you currently dating anyone?"

Phillip took another sip of his coffee. "The last girl I dated was in college. The girl who led me to Christ. How about you?"

"Nope. Still single. What happened to you and the girl from college?"

"After I accepted Christ, she wanted to move fast. Started talking about marriage and kids, and I was struggling to survive my next class."

"Women," he said jokingly.

Phillip grinned. "Tell me about it."

"I heard a rumor about Casey recently."

"Yeah?"

"It had something to do with a company her dad handed over to her. Something bad, like she lost it, or screwed it up somehow. I don't remember all the details, but it makes me wonder if she's in town because she's hiding out until the smoke clears," Scott said.

"Where did you hear that?"

Scott furrowed his brow. "My brother Parker, possibly. He works in Washington state and seems to know things like that. So, do you actually need to head out, or were you trying to get Casey to leave?"

"I wanted Casey to leave. I have been trying to stay close to the house in case Mom needs me, but other than that, I don't have anywhere I need to be."

"How's your mom really doing? I heard she was in the hospital."

He hesitated, still unsure how much to share. But Scott was a good guy. Even though they'd gotten into a lot of trouble when they were younger, he'd always been able to trust Scott not to blab all his secrets.

"That's actually why I'm in town. She was in the hospital for overdosing on sleeping pills, which she claims was an accident. My uncle is worried about her and is convinced she's depressed, but denying it. Richard thinks taking care of Grandma is getting to be too much for her, but she seems determined to keep at it."

"Oof, that's rough. But your mom seems okay since she's been home?"

"I think the verdict is still out on that."

Scott nodded. "If you're still around and aren't busy on Saturday, I'm having a beach day at the lake with the kids I mentor. We're going to have kayaks, paddle boards, swimming, volleyball, and I'm trying to get a couple of those water jet-pack things, too. It's going to be a blast. You should come."

"Wow, two invitations in less than ten minutes. I was never this popular in school."

Scott laughed. "Yeah, but one will be much more awesome than the other."

"I have no doubt. If things are good at the house and I can find a swimsuit, I'll come."

"Sweet," Scott said.

Chapter 10

"What the—?" Philip muttered to himself for the thousandth time as he sifted through pages of code on his laptop. Dan wasn't kidding about the back end of the app being a nightmare. They'd put their other business partner in charge of most of the tail-end work, but when he left, Dan thought he could handle taking on the task. Phillip had worked on it for six hours already today and was still having trouble making sense of it all. There seemed to be a lot of code that didn't go anywhere or mean anything scattered throughout.

Mom appeared in the kitchen doorway near the table and cleared her throat. He looked up at her. She fidgeted with the hem of her Pink Floyd shirt. "Grandma wants something to eat. I know it's early for dinner, but I thought I would see if you're hungry as well. I can whip up some sandwiches really quick if you are."

"Yeah, that sounds great. Thanks."

She nodded and headed to the fridge. He sat facing the kitchen, his back to the wall, and he watched her for a moment as she grabbed bread, lunch meat and other sandwich fixings and placed them on the counter. The past two days, Mom had helped Grandma get up, dressed, and fed, but once finished, disappeared into her room most of the day, coming out only to attend to Grandma's needs. He'd knocked on her door when he left to meet Scott yesterday, but saw nothing of her until she came out to prepare dinner. Today had been exactly the same.

What had she been doing? And was she hiding from him? Or just giving him space and quiet to do his work?

He looked at his computer screen, saved his work, and shut down the program. It was a good time for a break, so he went to check on Grandma.

Closing the laptop as he got up from his seat, he picked up the device and tucked it under his arm. In the living room, Grandma dozed in her oversized armchair. Her eyes were mostly closed but fluttered slightly. He rested his hand lightly on her arm, and she jerked her head up. "What? What is it? What's happened?" she asked, sounding alarmed.

"Nothing, Grandma, everything's fine. I wanted to see how you are doing and if you need anything."

She gave him a confused look for a moment. "Why am I all wet?"

He removed the small blanket resting over her knees and immediately knew she'd lost control of her bladder. "Why don't we go get you changed and cleaned up?"

Grandma covered her mouth with her hands and whimpered.

"It's all right. It's just a minor accident."

"What's an accident?" Mom asked, walking into the living room wiping her hands on a dish towel. She glanced over the chair and saw the wet stain on Grandma's pants. "Mom, I asked you to put on an adult diaper when you got dressed this morning. You can't keep dressing yourself if you won't put on what I set out for you." She tossed the towel on the back of Grandma's chair and took the blanket completely off her lap.

"I thought I did. I'm sure of it," Grandma said in a high-pitched, whining voice.

"I can help her with this, Mom," Phillip said, concerned at his mother's tone of voice.

Andi hesitated. "No, I should do it. She's more comfortable with me," she said, softening her tone. "Come on, Mom, let's clean you up."

Grandma nodded, but whimpered again.

"It's okay, Mom," Andi said, holding Grandma by one hand to help her out of the chair, and rubbing her back with the other. "We'll get you cleaned up and then we'll forget it ever happened."

They headed down the hallway. Phillip checked the chair for wetness. After setting his laptop on the couch, he headed to the kitchen and grabbed a cleaner from under the sink. He dabbed the fabric with a dry cloth, then sprayed the cleaner. While it did its work, he took the towel and blanket to the laundry room and tossed them into the washer. Then he blotted the wet spot with a clean towel, added that to the washer as well and started the machine. After washing his hands he returned to the kitchen, where he was shortly joined by the women.

"Okay, let's eat," Andi said. "Mom, why don't you go take your seat and I'll bring you a plate."

Grandma nodded and shuffled over. Phillip followed her and held her hand as she sat down to make sure she didn't lose her balance, while Mom carried their plates and drinks in her experienced waitress way and set them down, spilling nothing.

They ate in silence. Phillip noticed Mom was picking at her food and not really eating. She seemed distracted.

"Is everything okay, Mom?"

She let a small piece of bread crust fall to her plate and looked at him. "Yeah, why?"

He shrugged. "You're not eating, and you seem to have something on your mind."

She cleared her throat and shifted in her seat. "I do need to discuss something with you."

He furrowed his brow. "Okay."

She took a deep breath and averted her gaze. "I've been speaking with your father."

He froze and stared at her. Fiery anger rose inside him, to a degree he hadn't felt since he was a teen. "What?" he asked in a low voice.

Mom cleared her throat again but still wouldn't look at him. Instead, she stared at her mostly full plate and rolled bread crumbs between her finger and thumb. "We've been talking …" She quickly glanced up and him, then away. "Only on the phone," she added quickly. "He wants to see you while you're in town."

The words filtered through his brain, but he couldn't make sense of them. Why would Jake want to see him? How did Jake even know he was here? Why was Mom speaking with him?

"How long?" he asked.

"How long what?"

"How long have you been speaking with Jake?" he said slowly, trying to keep his anger from exploding. His hands shook, and he clenched them under the table.

Mom shifted nervously in her seat. "About a year."

"What?" he yelled and leaped out of his seat. "Why? Why are you talking to him again? Why?"

A year. They'd been talking for a year. Why? How had he convinced her to talk to him again? What lies had he used this time? He was pacing, his feet trying to keep up with the thoughts and questions racing through his mind. But Mom hadn't answered. He stopped in front of the table, rested his palms on the smooth surface, and looked at her. "Why?" he demanded.

Her eyes met his, and they pleaded with him. "He's turned his life around. He's been clean for three years now. We just talk. Not about anything serious. Our day. You."

He started pacing again and ran both his hands through his hair. This couldn't be happening. Of all the reasons he had for not wanting to come home again, Jake was number one. And Mom knew that. A horrible thought crossed his mind, and he turned to face her again. "Are you back together?"

Andi stood and rounded the table. "No. We're not back together, but we are friends." She rested a hand on his arm. "Please, Phillip, this is the longest your father has been clean, and he really has gotten his life together. He has partial ownership of the mechanic shop he's been working at. He's doing so well, and he wants a chance to apologize to you."

"Apologize." He spat the word out. "Nothing he could say could make amends for all the crap he did. To both of us. Mom, you can't trust him. You know he'll say anything to worm his way back in." And he wondered what kinds of things Jake had been telling his mother for the last year. Words that would undermine her self-confidence? Make her feel bad about herself? Things that could lead her to attempt suicide?

She dropped her hand and closed her eyes. "I told him you would be angry."

"But he pushed you to ask anyway, didn't he? What else has he said to you, Mom? Is he the reason you took those sleeping pills?"

Her mouth dropped open, and she shook her head. "No. Phillip, God no. I told you that was an accident. Your father had nothing—"

"Stop." He held up a hand. "Stop calling him my father. I may share genes with the man, but he was not a father." He shook his head. "I need to get some air." He turned and walked out of the house.

The center of town was three blocks from his grandmother's, and he arrived there before he even realized which direction he'd gone when he left the house.

His anger had subsided but hadn't left completely. Jake had promised him he would leave Mom alone before he left for college. It was the only reason he'd felt comfortable leaving and the only time he'd put his foot down with the man. The impression he'd left had been obvious, and he had felt certain that, despite not being able to keep any promises to him, ever, Jake would actually keep this one. But apparently there was no keeping those two apart. No matter how detrimental it might be to Mom or himself.

He looked around, trying to decide where to go. The town was busy this evening, as it usually was in the spring once the chill of winter had finally gone away. Tulips and daffodils bloomed everywhere, and so did every ornamental tree. But he didn't want to be around people right now. Didn't want to be stopped or chatted with. He wanted a quiet place to figure out how to deal with his family.

The beach would be full of people; the town wasn't safe. He decided to head east toward the open country, where it was just farms and fields. He might see cyclists and joggers, but no one who would want to stop and chat with him. Stuffing his hands in his pockets, he took off in that direction at a quick pace, his eyes focused on the ground in front of him.

"Phillip?"

He'd made it a block before the melodious sound of a woman's voice called to him. He looked up. Casey strolled toward him, grinning, and he groaned inwardly.

"Phillip, you didn't come to my party last night," she said with a pout on her red lips. Today her blond hair cascaded in loose, bouncy curls around her shoulders, and she wore an off-white summer dress with six-inch heels to match.

"Yeah, I couldn't make it." He started walking again, and she matched his stride.

"I wanted to talk to you about what you're doing with your business degree."

He glanced at her. "Now really isn't a good time."

"Yes, I can see you're a tad irritated. I'm guessing family issues?"

He didn't respond.

"It's always family, isn't it?"

He glanced at her and picked up his pace.

"Never mind that. I really don't care." She grabbed his arm and stopped walking, forcing him to do the same. "What I do care about is what you're doing with your business degree."

"Why?"

She stepped close to him, her nose nearly touching his. She grabbed his chin lightly with her finger and thumb. "I asked first." She spoke in a low, playful tone.

He gazed into her blue, almond-shaped eyes rimmed with black eyeliner, and smelled her fragrant perfume. She was trying to be intoxicating, trying to seduce and overwhelm him with her beauty, but he hadn't forgotten the way she'd treated him, and while it was unnerving to have her this close to him again, he wasn't about to fall for it.

But he also knew that once she attached herself to something, it was hard to shake her off. She wasn't prying into his family's situation, and answering her question might relieve his curiosity to know what she was up to, as well as distract him from the situation at home.

Casey seemed to sense that her flirtation wasn't working and stepped back and crossed her arms over her chest. The smile vanished and was replaced by a slight frown and an arched brow.

"I create apps," He said finally.

She grimaced. "Building them yourself, or working for someone else?"

"I work for myself."

She pursed her lips, narrowed her eyes, and sighed. After a moment, she asked, "Have you considered opening a brick-and-mortar store?"

"No."

Casey rolled her eyes and grabbed his arm. "Come with me."

He pulled his arm out of her grasp. "What is this all about, Casey?"

"Follow me and I'll show you," she said in an annoyed tone. "And on the way, you can explain why you've never considered opening an *actual* business."

"Do you have any idea how huge the app market is?" he asked, following her reluctantly.

"Yeah. I also know a lot of areas in the app market are over saturated. Unless you're developing the next great addictive game, I doubt you're making much money." She gave him a once-over. "You don't look like the gaming type."

It irritated him that she had pegged him so easily, and he chose not to respond.

After a few minutes, Casey stopped and waved her hand toward a small, old, two-story brick structure.

"It's a building," he said.

She dropped her hands and let them slap against her sides. "Duh. It's also beautiful, near the center of town, and has been sitting empty for years."

"What does this have to do with me?"

She moved close to him again, her hands on her hips. "This building is perfect for a luxury spa. Think about it, people visit from all over, all year round, and they stop at the coffee shop—"

"That your family owns."

Casey rolled her eyes. "Yes, that my family owns. Or eat at one of the restaurants."

"In the buildings your family owns."

She huffed. "Yes. They go to the ski resorts, play on the lake and hang out in the park. But there isn't anywhere to relax and unwind afterwards. A spa would give them that. Plus, think of all the wedding venues up here. Brides could get their hair and makeup done, and get pampered before the wedding."

"It sounds great. I still don't see where I come into this."

She turned her back on him, walked up to the building, faced him again, and placed her well-manicured hand on the window. "The owner refuses to sell. It's such a waste, this beautiful building sitting here empty. I thought you might convince the owner to sell it."

"And what would entice me to do this?"

"Are you really that dense? Of course we'd go into business together, dummy."

"Why don't you convince him?"

She cocked her head to the side. "I've tried."

"Me trying will make a difference because …?"

"Because you're a local. You grew up here."

He stared at her, waiting for more.

Casey rolled her eyes. "He's a local, you're a local; it's a weird thing this town has. They don't like dealing with outsiders."

He nodded slowly. "Outsiders who take over lots of land and develop like crazy when the people who live here prefer wide open spaces?"

"Yeah, something like that."

He stepped up to the building and cupped his hands to one of the large windows. Of course she wanted to use him to get something she wanted, but it couldn't be that simple. There was more to her story. No way she would make a fair deal with him.

It was empty, but everything looked in good condition. He tried to remember what the place had been, but couldn't. What Casey said was true. The building was beautiful. But partnering with her?

He turned and faced her. "So they won't sell to you because you're Casey Calloway and your family already owns half the town?"

"Yeah."

"You think because I grew up here they'll change their mind if I go into business with you?"

"If you present it as though you're the face of the company and I'm just an investor, yes."

He shook his head. She wanted to hide behind him, deceive the guy. "No thanks. I have too much going on right now already, and I'm not planning on moving back here to run a business."

"Ugh, please. Do I have to spell everything out for you? You don't have to move to run the place. That's why you hire managers."

He shook his head. Nothing she'd said had tempted him to accept. Partnering with Casey Calloway just seemed too risky.

"Look, I don't know why you're here, or what your family situation is, or why you were taking a walk to cool off just now, but if we can secure this building, I can bring in a team of people to get us up and running in six months. I don't know your financial situation, but I doubt you'd shake your head at extra income six months from now."

From flirting to money. Could she really turn this place around in such a short amount of time? His eyes ran over the face of the building. Even if it were true that she could get the place operational in six months, working with Casey still had risk.

"I don't think so. Sorry." He turned to leave, but she jogged up to him and grabbed his arm again. "At least consider it." She held out her business card.

"You already gave me one of those."

"And I'm sure you kept it, right?" She smirked.

He sighed, took the card, and put it in his back pocket.

Chapter 11

"Hello?" Richard ducked out of the living room, where his small group leadership team was gathered. They were having their monthly meeting to report on their groups and any issues that needed addressing and receive further training, prayer, and fellowship.

"Richard, I need your help," Andi said, sounding agitated.

"What's up?" Denise glanced at him from where she sat, a concerned expression on her face. She'd taken over when his phone rang and he excused himself. He tried to return her gaze with a reassuring one, but the tone of Andi's voice had him worried.

"You were upset that Jake stopped by while I was in the hospital. I spoke with Jake on Sunday to assure him I was okay. He wants to see Phillip while he's here. I told him I didn't think Phillip would agree to that, but he insisted he needed to apologize for the past. So, I told Phillip about Jake's call this afternoon, and he flipped out. He left the house about an hour ago and hasn't come back yet."

Richard leaned against the kitchen counter laden with snacks and finger foods. "What do you want me to do?"

"I want you to talk to Phillip. He listens to you, and you can convince him that Jake's intentions are good."

He hesitated and glanced at Denise, who was going through a suggested activity to help defuse tense situations. The irony wasn't lost on him. "I can't do that, Andi."

"Why not?"

"Because I don't know if I believe Jake's intentions are good."

"Unbelievable. I told you Jake has been clean for three years. Three years! But you can't accept that he's bettering himself because of your self-righteous, religious, judgmental beliefs."

"Andi—"

"No, I should have known you wouldn't believe Jake could change, or be able to forgive him, even though your religion tells you that's exactly what you're supposed to do. And you've dragged Phillip into it, too."

"Andi, Phillip being upset with Jake has nothing to do with Christianity. And I'm not the one who's been talking to Jake for the last year. I'm only aware of what you've told me in the last few days. You can't expect me to accept that Jake is a changed man in such a short time. Not after all those years of neglect and abuse. And you can't expect Phillip to accept it, either."

"He can't accept it if he won't try," she yelled.

"No, he can't. But he may not be ready to try. He hasn't dealt with the pain he endured as a kid."

"Don't start preaching to me about my son's pain. I did everything I could to protect him and make sure he felt loved."

"I know you did, Andi. And I'm not preaching, I'm just saying, Jake wounded Phillip deeply and Phil's been avoiding that pain. To have it come up again so suddenly—"

"Stop. I don't need you telling me how screwed-up my kid is because of Jake. I was there. I lived it, too. If you won't talk to Phillip, then I'll figure something else out."

"Andi—" But she'd already hung up. He sighed and stared at his phone. How had he messed up so badly with his own sister? If anyone should have seen Christ's love in him, it should have been her.

Now he had to return to the meeting when all he really wanted to do was take a walk around the property and try to figure out how he messed up so royally.

Straightening, he rolled his shoulders and rejoined the group.

"Everything okay?" Denise asked.

They had made a point of being open and authentic with their church members, but he didn't feel like sharing this latest crisis with them. Especially since it involved his sister and nephew. They hadn't given their consent to have their lives talked about and probably wouldn't appreciate it.

"Andi and Phil seem to be having a disagreement."

Denise raised an eyebrow and bit her upper lip.

"Anything we can pray for, Pastor?" asked Beth Dixon, wife of one of the local sheriffs. "It looks like that call really took the wind out of your sails." Her husband, Daniel, rarely made it to the group meetings because of his schedule and wasn't here today. The couple was supportive of all the changes he'd made. And she was a prayer warrior if he'd ever seen one; she never missed Denise's prayer group and occasionally took over when Denise couldn't lead it.

"I appreciate that." He gave her a half smile. "Yes, you can pray for wisdom for all of us as we navigate our current situation, and healing for all involved."

"But especially for our nephew, Phillip," Denise added.

Several people nodded and jotted the prayer request down in their notebooks.

"I saw Phillip with Heather and Scott at church this past Sunday," Beth said, looking thoughtful. "I wish I'd had a chance to talk with him after, but he skipped out pretty quickly."

"Yes, he wanted to get back to help Andi with my mother."

"Well, I hope I get to say hello at least, but if not, will you pass my greetings to him?"

"Of course," Richard said. "Now, where have we gotten to?"

After everyone left, Richard went to his office to work on emails. At least, that's what he'd told Denise. Instead, he sat in his chair, his head back, eyes closed. A few minutes later, Denise tapped lightly on his door and opened it, holding a cup of coffee. He smiled at her.

Denise entered the room, set the coffee mug on his desk, and wrapped her arms around his shoulders. "Sounded like that call with Andi didn't go very well. From what I could hear of it."

"No, it didn't. And I haven't told Phillip about Jake's visit, either."

"So he was caught unaware."

"Yes. She wants me to convince Phillip to meet with his dad while he's here." He turned his head and kissed Denise's cheek. "I don't know if he's ready for that."

Denise straightened and gave him a sympathetic look. "I don't either, but of anyone he knows, you're the most likely to help him see he needs to deal with his pain instead of pushing it aside."

"Do you think we could have done more for Phillip when he was younger to help him avoid all this pain?"

"Oh, hun, don't torture yourself with what-ifs. We can analyze the past for the rest of eternity and find things we could have done differently, but we can't go back and change things. Maybe here and there we might have been conscious of a different path we could have taken, but mostly we didn't know any better."

He nodded. "You're such a wise woman, Denise. I love you."

She grinned at him. "I love you, too. I'll leave you be to get those emails finished." She winked before closing the door to his office.

He picked up his coffee and took a sip. It was decaf. He set it down again and rubbed a hand over his face and beard. He hated that his sister's opinion of him seemed to be entirely based on his faith. Did she really see him as a religious Pharisee, touting doctrine and looking down on everyone else because they didn't believe the way he did? He and Andi hadn't been particularly close growing up. But there was seven years between them. When he left for college, she'd only been in fifth grade. Her rebellion against their parents hadn't started until she reached high school. By then, he was living his own life. He'd spoken to his sister at his mother's request, but it hadn't done any good. And how could it? They'd never had much of a relationship.

But he was nothing like their father. Ed Barker was determined to raise his children to be godly, obedient, well-respected people who faithfully attended church. The men in starched white dress shirts, slacks, and perfectly polished dress shoes. And the women in prim and proper dresses of the correct length, who kept to their station at home and at church.

Appearance had been a big deal back then. It was considered disrespectful to the Lord to show up to His house in anything but your best clothes. But how they appeared on the outside wasn't the main issue.

Growing up, he and Andi had different expectations placed on them, and they both rebelled in their own way. Andi was expected to be seen and not heard, to be modest, quiet, and obedient. She was raised on the expectation that she would become a wife and mother; stay at home and raise her children. But Andi wasn't quiet, she was lively and adventurous and wanted to explore the world. She had run off and eloped with Jake to escape her miserable existence at home.

He'd been raised to be respectable, honest, and upstanding in the eyes of the world and for some reason to be those things you had to wear suits and ties, keep a clean shaved face and have a crew cut. When he accepted Jesus at Bible camp as a teenager, and really began to read his Bible, he started having doubts about some of the things he'd been taught. He hadn't accepted the old traditions despite accepting Christ and the life of a churchgoer. Choosing to believe God could be found in worship outside of a hymnal, and that many of the rules churches imposed were too strict, too demanding—and had nothing to do with having a relationship with the Father.

He'd become a pastor not to follow in his father's footsteps, but to preach the gospel and nothing but. He wanted people to press into Jesus, like the first believers in Acts had done. And for a while, he thought he'd been on the right track. People enjoyed giving up the old traditions of church for the most part. To actually show up as yourself, not as some polished, righteous person who had life all figured out already. But he must have missed something, or side-stepped along the way, because now his people were all complacent. They came to hear a message that made them feel good about themselves for another week. And his sister hated him and considered him to be just like their father.

"God, what have I done wrong? Where did I miss it and how can I fix it? I don't know how to encourage my nephew to deal with his past, but I believe he needs to. It's what's best for him, and you want the things that are best for us. So, Lord, please give me wisdom to know what to do and what to tell him. And if there is anything I can do to repair the damage in my relationship with my sister, please give me wisdom and understanding for that as well."

Chapter 12

The sun had set when Phillip returned home and dusk was quickly giving way to darkness, leaving a chill in the air that reminded him spring was just dawning in the little town. Inside, the house was dark except for the glow of the television. Grandma was asleep in the recliner in the living room. After turning off the TV, he tucked the blanket around her shoulders, paused and listened for any signs Mom was up and about, but the house was silent. He flipped on the kitchen light and glanced around. He checked her medicine. The evening ones were still in their container, which wasn't a surprise. It was still a little early for her to take them. But where was Mom?

He opened the door to her room and found it dark. Flipping the light switch, he glanced at her bed. Empty. She wouldn't have left Grandma by herself, would she? Where would she go? Would she have gone somewhere with Jake? A sense of panic rose in him at the thought.

He returned to the kitchen; he checked his phone for messages. There were none. He paced the living room floor, wondering what he should do. Grandma seemed fine. The clock on the wall told him it was nearly seven thirty, so she must not have been alone for too long. But if Mom left, where did she go, and why didn't she send him a message so he could come home to take care of Grandma? Probably because he'd been so angry. But she could have told Uncle Richard so he or Denise could be here.

He checked Mom's room again. Empty. As he closed the door, he paused. He'd heard something. A sniffle. He headed toward the closet where he'd heard the sound. A small band of light seeped out under the door, and he opened it.

Mom sat curled on the floor next to a large cardboard box, crying. Relief and concern flooded him.

"Mom?"

She looked up at him with red-rimmed eyes and wiped her nose on the sleeve of her shirt.

Phillip grabbed a tissue from her nightstand, knelt on the floor beside her, and handed it to her. "Are you okay? Why are you in the closet?"

Andi chuckled and blew her nose. "Grandma asked to see photos of when she was a little girl. I came in here to get them and found this box of your baby clothes, and I've been sitting here, remembering. When I was in grade school, Mom insisted on teaching me how to sew. I hated it. But after you were born and your dad wasn't around, I couldn't afford much, so I made your clothes." Her lips trembled as she fingered a tiny pair of overalls. "Sorry, I don't know why it's making me so emotional." She shoved the box back and wiped her eyes. "I should get those photos for your grandmother." She started to get up, but Phillip rested a hand on her arm.

"Mom, wait. I'm sorry for getting so angry."

Andi nodded. "I should have told you I'd been talking to Jake. I know you're angry with him, and I should have been upfront with you."

"I guess I don't understand why *you* aren't angry. Why you don't hate him after all he did to you."

She reached over, placing her hand on the side of his face, and stroked his cheek with her thumb. "I know it's hard to believe, but I loved your dad at one time. We had a lot of fun before we got married. He was my best friend." She removed her hand and glanced at the pile of baby clothes. "The drugs and alcohol turned him into something we all hated. Even him." She looked back at him. "His childhood was rough, he never knew his dad, his mom was an alcoholic and barely paid him any attention. His circle of friends were the kind who committed crimes and did drugs. He never had positive influences." She gave him a sad smile. "He's really been trying, the past few years, and I've seen glimpses of the man he always wanted to be. I really wish you'd at least consider talking to him."

They were both silent for a moment. Phillip had never heard about his dad's past, had never thought to ask. But it didn't change anything. He'd still been absent most of his childhood, and when he wasn't absent, Jake was getting into trouble. He looked at the box, then at his mother. "I didn't know you made my baby clothes."

She smiled sadly and nodded.

"You don't have to protect me anymore, Mom. I'm an adult. I can handle whatever's making you so sad."

She shook her head and wiped at her eyes. "I need to find those pictures."

"Grandma's asleep. Tell me more about the clothes. Please?"

Andi sighed and leaned against the closet wall. "There's not much else to tell. I made most of your clothes until you were about three years old." She pulled the box out and picked out a red shirt and handed it to him.

He took it and inspected it, finding it hard to believe he used to fit into it. He fingered the hem of the shirt. "It looks like you were pretty good at it. I wouldn't have guessed it was homemade." He handed the shirt back to her.

"Yeah, who would have thought I would have a talent for doing something I absolutely hated as a kid?" She gave him a wry smile.

"Why did you keep them? You could have given them away when you moved in here."

She shrugged. "Sentimental value, I guess."

"Does Grandma know you made all this?"

Andi shook her head. "I don't think I ever told her. We weren't on speaking terms then, and by the time we were, I wasn't making your clothes anymore, so it never came up." She sighed. "I never thanked her for teaching me all the things she did when I was growing up. All of them—the sewing, cooking, cleaning—they were exactly what I needed to make it through those first few years after your dad was arrested." She sighed. "I fought my parents on everything. Their rules were so restrictive and religious, at least for me. Richard had it much easier, being a boy. I wanted nothing to do with their lifestyle. What does that verse say … If someone among you sins, cut them off? Dad used that verse when he told me he disowned me after Jake and I ran off to Vegas and eloped." Tears filled her eyes.

Phillip's gut twisted in disgust. He couldn't imagine anyone feeling that way about their own child.

"Mom was always there for me, though. Even when Dad forbade her from talking to me, she would occasionally send little notes with cash inside, or a gift card. Once, after you were born, I ran into her at the grocery store and she cooed over you for a good five minutes." Tears streamed down her face again, and she wiped at them with the tissue. "She wanted to hold you, I could tell. But she didn't ask, and I was so angry, and stupid, and stubborn that I didn't offer. I never thanked her for being there for me, even when I didn't want her there. And now it's too late. She doesn't know who I am most of the time." Andi buried her head in her arms and sobbed.

Phillip rubbed her arm. Was it possible that Mom was trying to make up for things she regretted as a child and young adult? He had no idea how many regrets she was holding onto, but seeing her sitting in the closet sobbing like this made him aware that it was a very heavy burden for her to carry. How could he help her let go?

"Is that why you don't want Grandma in a nursing home?"

Andi wiped her face but didn't look at him. "I can't fail her again."

"Mom, you haven't failed Grandma. You've taken great care of her. But I know you've been struggling with depression."

She looked up at him accusingly, and he paused.

"Mom, come on. You're not yourself. What else am I supposed to call it?"

She closed her eyes and blew out a breath.

"Would you rather I was in California right now? Not knowing that you're struggling?"

She opened her eyes. "I only want you to be happy, not stuck like I am. Like I've always been."

He tried swallowing back the guilt rising in him. That's exactly why he'd left, so he wouldn't end up stuck like his parents. Only, he'd intended on being successful and providing for his mom so she wouldn't have to stay stuck, either. So far, he hadn't been able to do that. Partnering with Casey might change that; give him enough money to invest in his next idea and help Mom.

Andi reached out and cupped his face in her hand again. "I'm so proud of you for going to school and pursuing your dreams and goals."

He reached over and picked up a little pair of overalls. "Did you hate having to make all these?"

She fingered the pant leg. "No. I think it's because I was making them for you, but I learned to love sewing. In fact, I miss it sometimes." She smiled at him, and he smiled back.

"I know you don't like that Jake and I have been talking, but I promise I'm being careful. He has changed," Andi said.

Phillip raised his eyebrows and sighed.

"He hasn't tried to win me back. He just wants to talk. Mostly about you. He's full of regrets."

"I can't imagine why," Phillip said sarcastically.

"He's not expecting any kind of relationship with either of us, but he wants to apologize to you."

Phillip nodded and rubbed his hand over his face. "Okay, okay. I'll think about it."

Grandma called out for help and Phillip stood, offering a hand to Mom to help her up. "Maybe you should start sewing again."

She chuckled. "What would I make?"

He shrugged. "Make baby clothes and sell them online."

Andi paused at the door of her room. "Maybe," she said unconvincingly. "Help me with your Grandma?"

He nodded and followed her out of the room. After helping Mom get Grandma ready for bed, he sent Casey a quick text message.

I may reconsider a business deal,
but want to see your offer before deciding.

Her reply was almost instantaneous.

I'll have something drawn up by next week. <3

Chapter 13

A cool breeze rippled the water on the lake. Phillip grabbed the bag he'd packed with a beach towel and sunscreen before shutting the trunk.

He made his way down a rocky path to the beach, where he could see Scott and a group of about twenty teenagers grouped around several paddle boards and kayaks. After his disappointing phone call with Dan this morning, he'd almost decided not to come today, but Mom had decided to clean the whole house this afternoon and he'd felt in the way.

As he approached, the group dispersed, several claiming one or another of the floating devices and heading for the water. The others either headed out to swim, or laid towels and blankets on the sand and applied tanning lotion before lying down to soak up the sun.

Scott stood near a man who was attaching a water jet pack to a teenager. A few of the kids stood nearby, presumably waiting to use it. Heather was there, too. His stomach lurched at the sight of her. She wore a light blue tankini top and had a black sarong wrapped around her waist. Her dark brown hair hung loosely around her face. He hadn't realized she would be here too, and he suddenly felt self-conscious in the cheap, black-and-white checkered swim trunks he'd picked up in town this morning. It was a ridiculous pattern, but at the store he'd grabbed the first pair in his size, along with a few shirts so he wouldn't have to keep washing and wearing the same two he'd brought with him. Now he wished he'd taken more time to choose.

"Hey," he said as he drew near.

The group all turned to look at him, Scott and Heather grinning while the teens gave him a once-over and then focused their attention back on the water toy.

"Hey man," Scott said, raising his arm for a bro handshake. Phillip matched the gesture, and their hands slapped together. Scott pulled him in for a quick hug and they thumped each other's backs. "Glad you could make it."

"Okay, you're all set. Let's get you in the water and practice a few things before we get you airborne," the instructor said.

The teen nodded and headed awkwardly toward the reservoir with the large pack strapped to his back.

"I didn't know those jet pack things came with an instructor, but after watching the videos on how to use it, I'm sure glad it does," Scott said, unfolding a towel and laying it out on the sand.

Heather already had her towel on the ground and was sitting on it, her legs stretched out, the sarong showing off a well-toned calf and part of her thigh.

Phillip laid his towel out next to Scott and took a seat.

"Scott," yelled a teen.

"Yeah?"

"Are you gonna sit there all day or you gonna get out here? You promised us a race."

Scott grinned and looked at Phillip. "Wanna go beat some teenagers in a swimming race?"

"I think I'll sit this one out. Wait for it to warm up." He rubbed his arms. If the breeze died down, the weather would be perfect, but there was a slight chill in the air that made the notion of getting into a lake full of recent snow melt an unpleasant one.

"I agree," Heather said. "You're all crazy."

Scott scrambled to his feet. "Wimps." And he took off running toward the water.

Phillip and Heather both laughed and watched Scott dive in headfirst and come up hollering from the cold.

They continued to watch Scott and the teenagers playing as an awkward silence stretched between them. He wanted to talk to her, and look at her, but his mind was blank of every topic save how dumb he looked in these swim shorts. So he kept his eyes on the people in the lake, even though the figure near him absorbed his thoughts. He tried to remember everything Scott had told him about Heather when they'd had coffee, and his mind finally kicked into gear.

"Scott told me you're going for a master's degree," he said, looking over at her.

She blew out a breath. "That's the plan."

"So you'll be Heather Fletcher, Horse Whisperer MBA?" he said, regretting the words as they came out of his mouth. It was dumb. He was dumb for saying it.

But she laughed. "Something like that. It might be MS for Master of Science, but I want to focus on animal-assisted therapy, so I haven't decided yet what master's program I'm going to work toward."

He nodded. "What made you choose this path?"

"I realized there were families who needed support that couldn't get it anywhere else, and I have a gift with horses that I can use to help fill some of that need." She sat up straighter and folded her arms. "At least, I hope I can. Sometimes I wonder if all this work I'm doing will actually result in filling that need gap."

"Why wouldn't it?" he asked, feeling a little more at ease with her admission of doubt. He'd always seen her as confident, always knowing exactly what she wanted and why. Certain it was the right choice. As a lost and wandering teenager, he'd been intimidated by that. But now, here she sat, admitting to him, of all people, that she had doubts and fears, like he did. And he wanted to assure her she would make a difference. She had made the right choice. Even if he didn't fully understand what path she was on.

She shrugged. "I want to help people who have invisible disabilities. People who appear normal on the outside, but struggle on so many levels. There is a lot we still don't understand about many of these disabilities, and I can only hope the research I'm doing today and will continue to do over the years will be enough to create a difference. It probably sounds ridiculous, and maybe a little self-righteous, but I want to make a difference *now*. I know the research I, and others, do now will benefit future generations, but I don't want that to be the only thing I succeed at. If that makes sense."

He nodded. It made perfect sense. Only in his situation, he needed to make life better for the past generation—his mom. Of course, he wanted his own family too, and his success would then benefit the future generations. But the idea was the same. Their desire was to help correct a wrong and see the benefits in their lifetime.

"Would your horse therapy program help someone with depression?" He was pretty certain he would never convince Mom to try regular therapy, let alone horse therapy, but it couldn't hurt to learn about it.

"Are you depressed?" she asked, sounding only half serious.

He chuckled. "No, but I think my mom is."

The half-smile on her face became a frown. "I'm sorry." She looked like she wanted to say more, but hesitated and looked across the reservoir. She returned her gaze to him. "Is that why she was hospitalized?"

It was his turn to look away, but he nodded. He watched a teen zoom over the lake, two spouts of water shooting from the bottom of the jet pack. "She overdosed on sleeping pills." He returned his gaze to her face to catch her reaction. There was no shock there, only the same sympathetic look she'd had before. "She keeps saying it was an accident, but my uncle isn't so certain, and I don't really know what to think at this point."

She scooted herself onto Scott's towel, then reached over and squeezed his arm. The contact sent an electric current up his arm, and his heart beat faster. She released her grip and wrapped both her arms around her knees. "Animal therapy is great for treating depression," she said finally. "But therapy only works if the person is invested in their own healing."

He sighed. "Yeah, that's the problem, and why it's so confusing for me. She won't admit anything is wrong, and sometimes I can't tell if there is."

"One thing I've learned over the last four years is that often the person with the invisible disability isn't the only person hurting. It tends to be a whole family issue, because so much work has to go into caring for the individual, or everyone is walking on eggshells so they don't upset the individual."

He considered the past week. He'd nearly convinced himself a dozen times things were fine and he could leave. But somehow, leaving didn't feel right yet. He just couldn't figure out why. "I guess I can understand that. But it almost seems like Mom is walking on eggshells around me, more than I am her."

She turned toward him. "Hmm ... sounds like she doesn't want you to worry."

"Yeah. Or she thinks she's protecting me somehow."

She nodded thoughtfully. "I hold group sessions every Tuesday and Thursday evening. You're welcome to come check it out and observe. Maybe you can talk your mom into coming too."

He doubted his mother would go for that, but an opportunity to observe Heather at work and possibly learn something that could help Mom was a win-win in his book. "Thanks, I'll definitely keep that in mind."

Scott walked up the beach toward them, water streaming down his body. Heather returned to her towel as he approached, and he collapsed between them, panting.

"Who won?" Heather asked.

"Not me," Scott said. "Not even once."

"How does that make you feel, big brother?"

He grinned and looked over at his sister. She had that half joking, half serious look on her face again. "Old and tired."

He sat up and pointed out at the lake. "You see those kids over there, playing chicken?"

"Yeah," they both said in unison and grinned.

"I used to be the one sitting on someone else's shoulders. Now I'm just the old guy that gets picked to be sat on."

Phillip laughed.

"But that means they still see you as strong," Heather said, grinning.

Scott shoved her playfully. "Stop psychoanalyzing me." Scott looked at Phillip. "Watch out for that. She does it a lot."

Heather returned the shove, blushing. "I do not."

"Heather, I saved us a kayak," a younger girl said, jogging up to them. She looked to be about thirteen. "Are you ready to go with me?"

Heather stood up and shook the sand from her sarong. "Yes, let's go."

The girl did a little hop and grabbed onto Heather's arm, half dragging her down the beach.

"Some of the kids want to start a volleyball game. Care to join?" Scott asked.

"Sure." They got up and headed to a section of beach that had three volleyball courts. You had to bring your own net, but otherwise, they were available for anyone who frequented the beach to use.

After an hour, he and Scott headed back to their towels out of breath and sweaty, along with most of the teenagers. Heather and a few girls were already there, sunbathing and chatting. "Who wants to grab the coolers from Heather's truck?" Scott asked.

A few of the boys volunteered and made off toward the parking lot.

Phillip sat down on his towel and watched his old friend interact with the kids. Amazed at how comfortable they all seemed, how easily they joked with him and seemed to trust him. He wondered how his childhood might have been different if he'd had someone like Scott in his life. If he would have felt less alone in the world. He thought about what Mom had said about Jake. How might *his* life have turned out if he'd had someone like Scott?

"Have you ever considered becoming a youth pastor?" he asked when there was a quiet moment.

Scott laughed. "Nah. Most of these kids would never step foot in a church. I enjoy being out here in the real world with them."

As soon as the two large coolers were placed on the ground, they were swarmed by teens grabbing paper bags of food from one and drinks from the other before retreating to their own blankets or towels and settling down into a tired but contented silence, with very little talking for the first several minutes.

Scott handed him a bag. "Hungry?"

He was starving, actually. "You sure you have enough?"

"Oh yeah, there's like ten more bags in the cooler."

He accepted the offered bag. "Thanks." Inside was a ham sandwich, apple slices, and a granola bar. He drew out the sandwich and unwrapped it from the plastic.

Scott resumed his seat on the towel next to him and dug into his own bag.

"So, I ran into Casey again," he said.

Scott raised his eyebrows. "What did she want this time?"

He took a bite of an apple slice, chewed, and swallowed it before answering. "She wants to open a luxury spa in the empty building on Third Street, and she wants me to be a partner in the venture."

"Casey Calloway?" Heather asked, leaning forward to see around her brother.

He nodded.

"Casey wants to go into business … with you," Scott said.

"Yeah, I know, weird."

"What did you say?" Scott asked sticking a whole apple slice in his mouth.

He watched his friend closely as he said, "I said no at first."

Scott coughed and pounded his chest. "At first?"

"I decided it couldn't hurt to look at a contract before I decided."

Scott froze mid-chew and narrowed his eyes. "You're actually thinking about it?"

He shifted uncomfortably. "It depends on what terms she comes up with. She claims she can get the place up and running in six months. I'm not so sure I believe that, but with my mom's health issues, it would be nice to have some extra cash to help her out if she needs it."

"Is that the place they used as the temporary library while they tore down and rebuilt the old one?" Heather asked.

Phillip thought for a moment. He hadn't been able to remember what the building used to be, but somewhere in the recesses of his mind, he seemed to recall the library moving while they rebuilt it. He'd never been a frequenter of the library, but he'd heard all the news about it. "I think so."

"That's a pretty small building for a luxury spa," Scott said. "Is she planning on tearing it down to build something new?"

Phillip shrugged. "It didn't sound that way. I can't imagine she'd be able to tear down, build a new building and get a business going in half a year." He eyed the brother and sister and couldn't tell if they were against the idea of him working with Casey, the luxury spa, or both.

"I'm not confident townsfolk will get behind the idea of a spa," Scott said carefully. "Aren't you in the middle of making an app or something?"

Phillip set the uneaten portion of his sandwich down on the plastic wrapping and wiped his hands on his towel. "One of my business partners dropped out a month ago, and the other has been thinking about quitting. He called this morning to tell me he was done, so this current project is dead unless I find a new partner or two. We've created a few apps together but haven't seen as much success as we hoped for when we started. It's got me thinking I should give up on apps and consider other options. Working with Casey isn't ideal, but it could give me some experience in a different area."

Scott nodded. "I guess that makes sense. Just be careful, man."

"I will."

As everyone finished eating, parents of the teens began to arrive. Phillip stayed to help pick up trash and pack the gear and coolers into Heather and Scott's vehicles. He wasn't sure if it was his imagination or not, but it seemed Heather had actively tried to avoid him after he told them about Casey's business proposition.

"Thanks for coming, man," Scott said, giving him another bro hug.

"Thanks for inviting me. I had fun. I think I needed it." He wanted to tell Heather he looked forward to attending her group session, but she had wandered off and was leaning against her truck, talking on the phone. He didn't want to appear desperate by waiting around until she was done with her call, so he headed to his car, glancing back at her before ducking inside.

Chapter 14

Richard stood near the main entrance of the church, shaking hands and wishing people a good rest of their week, hoping he'd just missed seeing his nephew in the crowd. But Phillip wasn't there, which meant something had probably happened at Andi's.

When most people had left the church, he retreated from his post and searched for Denise. She would be preparing for her post-service prayer group meeting. He headed toward the classroom she used for that purpose and found her rearranging chairs.

"I'm going to make sure everything is okay at Andi's."

Denise looked up at him. "Okay. Do you want to take some snacks with you? It looks like we have a small group today."

Richard shook his head.

"Hun, are you all right?"

He paused at the door. "Just worried about Andi and Mom."

"No, I know that. I mean, with everything else."

"What do you mean?"

"Church. You seem ... I don't know ... discouraged lately," she said.

He gave her a small smile. "I'm fine. Just tired."

Denise folded her arms. "Richard."

He sighed. "Let's talk about it later."

"I'm going to hold you to that."

He left, but backtracked and gave Denise a kiss. "Add our situation to the prayer list."

"I already have."

Climbing into his SUV, he drove the three blocks to Andi's house. He wondered when he'd started referring to his childhood home as Andi's house. Technically, the house still belonged to his mother, but after Andi moved in and took over Mom's care, it began to feel like hers. Even though she hadn't changed anything—the furniture was the same, the pictures on the walls were the same—she'd taken an ownership of the place that made it hers. And when Mom was gone, it would be hers—no matter what Mom and Dad's will said. He had his own place; he didn't need a second one. Besides, Andi had earned it. She'd faced enough challenges in her life and deserved to have a comfortable home she didn't have to worry about paying for. Mom and Dad had paid the house off years ago.

Parking, he climbed out and went to the door. He listened a moment but didn't hear anything, then knocked.

Phillip answered with a weary smile and invited him inside.

"What happened?" he asked. The living room was in chaos. Cushions were off the couch, picture frames knocked over, lap blankets strewn about the room, and books littered the floor. Mom sat in the oversized armchair sobbing, Andi attempting to console her.

"Grandma wanted a trinket box her father gave her when she was a child. She couldn't find it, became upset and tore half the house apart before we could get her to calm down to find out what she was looking for," Phillip said, picking a blanket up off the floor and folding it before placing it on the blanket rack next to the piano. "I already cleaned up the kitchen."

"And she's still upset?" he asked.

Andi glanced at him, her expression one of lingering annoyance. She was probably still mad at him over their conversation about Jake.

"Not about the trinket box," Phillip said. "She had an off day this morning. She got upset about breakfast being eggs instead of French toast, and didn't like the blouse Mom set out for her. I'm not certain what's got her upset now."

"Her favorite show isn't on," Andi said.

"What can I do?" he asked.

"You can help me finish cleaning up," Phillip said.

Richard nodded and headed toward the books on the floor.

Andi persuaded Mom to rest, and they got up, making their way slowly down the hall.

Richard returned the last book to the shelf and glanced at Phillip, who straightened pictures on the piano.

"If I'm going to be here a while, I should return my rental car and hitch a ride when I need it. Everything in town is pretty much walkable. I need a ride from the rental place, though. Would you or Denise be able to help me with that sometime this week?"

"We can make that work."

"Thanks."

They continued to clean in silence. Richard considered how to talk to his nephew about Jake. "Phil, I've been contemplating some things recently, and I'd appreciate your opinion."

"Okay."

"Where do you think the church is headed?"

Phillip stopped what he was doing and turned to look at his uncle. "What do you mean?"

"I mean, there aren't a lot of young people at church anymore. It makes me worry about the future, about how church is done, and if something needs to change."

Phillip looked thoughtful. "Well, there are things I've never liked, even after being saved."

"Like what?"

"The lack of participation, how it's always so difficult to find a group to belong to … at least it is for me. I often wonder why a church continues to offer certain programs when there aren't enough people willing to run them. Plus, I think people still feel they have to look and act a certain way. They can't appear too broken, so there is a lack of authenticity and genuine connection."

Richard sighed. He agreed with his nephew's assessment. "Do you think that's why young folks don't choose to come to church?"

"Yeah. Even Scott says he would rather mentor kids outside of church because they don't think they'd be welcomed. It's frustrating. Something needs to get people to view church as more than just a social club. There needs to be more purpose behind it."

"Why do you go if you find it so frustrating?"

Phillip shrugged. "Isn't that what we're supposed to do? The Bible says, don't forsake the gathering of yourselves together. I wish there was a different way of gathering together, but I haven't found alternates so far …" He trailed off.

Richard glanced at him as he set a small decorative bowl on the coffee table. Phillip regarded him thoughtfully.

"Actually, now that you mention it," Phillip continued, "I thought your service was pretty unique. I was engaged the whole time, and it seemed like most people were."

Richard placed a cushion back on the couch, then sat on it. "Did I share the changes I made with you?"

"Yeah, but I guess I haven't thought about it much, because it surprised me when I walked into the sanctuary. Didn't the changes have to do with some research you'd found on relationships?"

Richard nodded. "Yes, what relationships look like in the brain and the how they develop. We're supposed to be the body of Christ, living in relationship with one another, but we've created an institution instead. It's been that way since the Roman empire and when I read that research I felt I needed to try and change the focus back to being relational. But, despite the changes, I feel there is still something lacking. I'm considering retirement and feel like I need to figure it out so I can train someone to take over the church."

"Retire? What will you do if you retire?" Phillip placed the two other cushions in their spots and sat next to his uncle.

"Spend more time with Denise, travel. Get some horses again. I'm not sure; I'm tired. I don't have it in me anymore to run a church."

"You did look pretty tired last Sunday. Heather noticed, too, and asked if you were all right. Are you positive it's not just everything going on here?" Phillip asked, lowering his voice, and they both glanced down the hallway.

"Heather, huh?" he said, searching his nephew's face.

Phillip glanced away and covered his mouth.

Richard leaned back and decided not to pursue that subject. Phillip had always been infatuated with the Fletcher girl, but he trusted him not to get involved in any kind of romantic relationship on a temporary visit. "It's more than that. I've been trying to build a church full of people who have a relationship with Jesus. But I don't have that. I have a church who still, as you say, view Sunday morning as a social club and don't want to volunteer for outreaches or events. Somehow, I've failed my assignment as pastor and I don't know how to fix it this late in the game."

Richard looked at his nephew, who had a concerned expression on his face. He wondered why it was so easy to confide his doubts to Phillip but hadn't even been able to express them to his wife. He could see Phil was trying to come up with a response. He sat up and clapped his hand over Phillip's knee. "Speaking of figuring out how to fix things, I need to fix another issue."

Phillip raised his eyebrows. "What?"

"I think I made a mistake recently. Andi asked me to speak to you about your dad and I refused."

Phillip looked away from him. "I don't want to talk about Jake."

"That's okay, but at least hear me out."

Phillip drew his mouth in a tight line, but he nodded.

"When you arrived at the hospital, do you remember the call I received from Denise?"

"Yes."

"I told you Denise was having trouble with Grandma, but that was a lie. Jake showed up here."

Phillip stood, stuffed his hands in his pockets, and began pacing. "He was here? Why?" He kept his voice low, but Richard could tell it was an effort for him.

"I believe you know that your parents have been talking on the phone for a while."

"Yeah."

"Well, when Andi didn't answer the phone, he feared the worst and came to check on her. He told Denise Andi had said some things to him that had him worried."

Phillip stopped pacing and stood in the middle of the floor. "What kinds of things?"

"I'm not sure. He didn't want to break the trust he'd built up with her by blabbing."

Phillip rolled his eyes and began pacing again. "Why didn't you tell me? You asked me to come here and help, but then kept all this from me?" His agitation was increasing, but he kept his voice low and glanced toward the hallway frequently.

Richard wondered if Andi had figured out they were having the talk she'd requested him to have with Phil, or if she'd retreated to her room to hide. "I wasn't aware of this before you arrived. And I wasn't sure how to tell you about Jake. I know you carry a lot of pain from your childhood."

Phillip returned to the couch, resumed his seat, and buried his head in his hands. "Apparently, he wants to talk to me. Apologize."

"Yes, that's why your mom wanted me to talk to you. She thought I could convince you to agree to his request."

His nephew raised his head and looked at him.

"But I couldn't do that because I don't trust him."

"And now you've changed your mind?"

"No, but I have had time to consider. Who knows if your dad has really cleaned himself up or changed his ways, but your mom believes it, and trusts him enough to confide in him in ways she can't confide in either of us. And he showed up here worried about her wellbeing. I can't say I ever remember him doing that before."

"That's true."

"If there is a way you can talk to Jake to help your mom, then it would be worth it." He hesitated and rested his hand on his nephew's arm. "Phil, you also need to deal with the pain you've been carrying around. Maybe talking to Jake will begin that process for you. Get you to a place where you can forgive him, so you can heal."

Phillip nodded. "Mom told me about his past … his childhood. It doesn't change anything about my childhood, but … I guess it does help me understand him better. I don't know if I can forgive him, but I will consider talking to him … for Mom's sake."

Chapter 15

"Mom?" Phillip knocked lightly on Andi's bedroom door.

"Yeah?" came her soft, faraway voice, accompanied by the squeak of the bedspring mattress.

"Will you be okay with Grandma for a while if I go out, or would you rather I stay home tonight?"

The door opened a crack, and Mom peered out at him, looking tired and disheveled. "You go. We'll be all right. I was just taking a nap, but I'm up now."

He hesitated. "You're sure? I don't mind staying and helping."

She waved him off. "Go."

He nodded, and she shut the door.

Back in the living room, he wondered if he should stay, anyway. She'd taken refuge in her room more and more over the past few days, only coming out for Grandma's routine care needs. Yesterday he'd asked her why she spent so much time in her room, and she said she could hear Grandma better in there since their rooms were right next to each other. It would have made sense, except that Grandma often sat in the living room during the day.

Trying to walk as softly as possible, he went back down the hallway and listened at Mom's door. He could hear her moving around in there, so she hadn't gone back to bed at least. If she came out and found him still here, she might become upset. He checked his watch. If he was going to make Heather's group session on time, he needed to leave shortly. But leaving didn't feel right.

He returned to the living room and sat down. Heather had another group session on Thursday. He could attend that one. Tonight he would stay here.

A moment later, Mom came out, her hair brushed and pulled back into a ponytail. She wore a thick robe and thin slippers. "I thought you were heading out."

"I decided I'd rather stay here tonight."

Mom put her hands on her hips. "Phillip, I'm fine. Grandma's fine. Go, have fun doing whatever it is you're doing."

His heart twinged. She hadn't asked where he was going and didn't seem to care. Did she even want him here?

"Mom, really, I changed my mind."

"Phillip, get out of this house. You're young, you do not need to sit around here monitoring two boring old ladies. And since you've decided to stay longer than necessary, you may as well have some fun. We don't need a babysitter."

"I would hardly call you old, Mom." He tried to hide his disappointment. Apparently, she thought he'd overstayed his welcome. Perhaps it was time to think about heading home.

"Yeah, well, I sure feel it lately. Now please go. Have fun."

"Okay," he said, getting up from the couch. Since she was practically pushing him out of the house, he decided not to argue with her. He grabbed his keys from the kitchen counter. "But if you need anything, please call me. I'll come right back."

She nodded, and he turned to leave.

It took ten minutes to reach the Fletcher farm. He made his way down the long dirt driveway, and once he reached the fork in the road, followed the signs to Heather's Horse Rescue. He could see the house Heather and Scott grew up in. He remembered it well. But he wasn't headed in that direction. The house on the left belonged to Scott and

Heather's grandparents. He wondered if they were still alive or if Heather had moved to the white house.

As he parked, it was obvious she used the barn at least. A group of people and horses were gathered in a large, rectangular paddock in front of the old barn, and Heather was leading another horse out of the building and into the ring. He climbed out and headed her way.

Heather paused when she saw him. "You made it."

"Yeah, sorry I'm a little late," he said, admiring the all-black horse she was leading.

"No worries, we haven't gotten started yet, anyway." She opened the gate to the paddock and invited him to enter.

"Oh, I can watch from out here."

She grinned. "Nice try. You may only be here to observe, but this is a hands-on observation. Come on," she coaxed.

"Okay." He entered but stayed near the gate.

Heather led the horse through, dropping his lead and patting his side to encourage him to keep moving forward into the center while she closed the gate. He counted five families lined around the edges of the enclosed space. Each had their own horse.

"Welcome, everyone. Some of you have been to our group sessions before, and some of you are new to it. I designed this group as more of an introduction to the weekly group session that's held on Thursdays. I present basic skills and introduce specific skills and how they can help with different issues. It's also an opportunity for some of our clients who have been here longer—"

"Like me!" shouted a boy who looked to be about ten or eleven years old and who stood on the opposite side of the ring from Phillip.

Heather smiled. "Yes, exactly, like Xavier here. Xavier has been in our program from the beginning—well, actually, from before the beginning. He has done so well and has learned so much that I felt he needed another challenge, so I invited him and one other client here tonight to help me show what our group sessions are all about. For them, this is a continuation of their group sessions. They've been learning how to communicate and build trust with their horses, but now they also get to learn how to communicate and build trust with other people as well."

The boy, Xavier, jiggled his leg so much Phillip was surprised it hadn't come loose from his body.

"The first thing we want our horses to know is that we are in charge, not them. It's pretty important to communicate this, because these guys weigh about twelve hundred pounds each. Phillip, I'll have you work with Littlefoot and Xavier."

Phillip had been leaning against the fence panel, but he straightened and then pointed to himself. He wasn't certain he wanted to be used as the teacher's example.

"Yes, come on. Don't be shy." She smiled at him encouragingly.

Xavier ran up to him and tugged on his arm. "Come on! I'll show you exactly what to do. Littlefoot is my horse, and he listens so great. I promise, this is going to be soooo easy."

Phillip allowed Xavier to drag him toward the center of the paddock.

"See? Hold your hand out to him like this so he can sniff you. It tickles at first, but you'll get used to it."

Phillip obeyed and held his hand out. The big, black horse sniffed his open palm. Phillip gazed into his big brown eye and ran a hand over the side of his face. "He's a beautiful horse."

"That's because I brush him a lot and make his hair shiny," Xavier said.

"Okay, the first thing I want you to do is get to know your horse," Heather said. "I'm going to come around and give you each some treats. But I want you to walk around your horse, run your hands over their sides, run your hand through their tail—just be careful not to stand right behind your horse. We don't want anyone getting kicked. Run your hands down their legs, touch their ears and mane. Those of you new to horses might think this is a little scary. I promise you we have rigorously trained these horses for these classes. They are gentle giants."

Xavier stood in front of Littlefoot and gently tugged on his lead. The horse lowered his head so the boy could reach his ears and mane. Xavier stepped forward and scratched around Littlefoot's ears. "Here, I lowered his head so you can touch his ears and mane too."

Phillip smiled, impressed with both Littlefoot and the boy, and reached his hand out to stroke the horse's velvety ears.

"Great job, son," a dark-haired man standing nearby said.

Xavier beamed at him, then waved.

Phillip nodded at the man and the skinny blond woman standing next to him, who he assumed was the man's wife and Xavier's mother.

After giving Littlefoot a lip-smacking kiss between his eyes, Xavier gave the horse another cue and Littlefoot raised his head. Phillip followed the boy, exploring the powerful muscles as they went, amazed that a small boy like Xavier had such control over this large beast.

"Here are some treats for Littlefoot," Heather said. Xavier held out his hands and Heather dropped a couple of small carrots into them. Then she turned to Phillip and handed him a few as well. "How are you doing? Xavier isn't running circles around you, is he?"

Phillip shook his head. "No, he's pretty amazing, actually."

Heather looked tenderly toward Xavier, who was wiping his hands on his jeans after feeding Littlefoot the carrots. "Yeah, he is."

"Hey you, Littlefoot wants his treats now," Xavier said.

"Xavier, this is Phillip," Heather said. "If you can't remember someone's name, just ask, okay?" She tousled his hair and moved on to the next family.

"Phillip, Littlefoot wants his carrots now," Xavier repeated.

"Okay." He walked to Littlefoot's head and held his hand out. The horse scooped both carrots into his mouth at once. "Sorry I kept you waiting, big guy."

"Now that you've gotten to know your horses a little better, let's do a simple exercise. As I mentioned before, we want our horse to know we are in charge. So we're going to give our horses some basic commands. I'll show you what to do with Littlefoot here, and how to correct your horse if they don't listen. Xavier, I'm going to show this first command, and then you can show everyone the next one. Deal?"

The boy nodded his head vigorously.

"Great, so what you're going to do is stand in front of your horse with arms spread wide and you're simply going to walk toward them and say, 'Back.' Your horse should start walking backwards, their eyes and ears focused on you. If they refuse to move, or their focus wanders, you want to correct them with a loud 'Ach.' This is their cue that they aren't doing what you want and they need to pay attention. All right, let's see you all try it out."

"Okay, Phillip, you stand right here and I'll tell you what to do," Xavier said.

Phillip stood where the boy pointed and stretched his arms out.

"No, stand right. Here." Xavier leaned down and touched the dirt a couple of inches in front of him.

Phillip chuckled and took a small step forward.

"Now, put your arms a little higher."

He slowly raised his arms, watching Xavier's face.

"Okay, stop. Right there is perfect. Now walk forward and at the same time say 'back' to Littlefoot."

Phillip nodded at him and did as the boy instructed. Littlefoot didn't move. He tried again, but Littlefoot just stood there. He glanced around and saw everyone else's horses doing what they were supposed to.

"You have to make the noise. Ach, ach!" Xavier said, waving his arms up and down. Littlefoot stepped backwards.

"Okay, I'll try again." He hoped the horse would listen this time.

He stepped toward the horse, arms raised. "Back," he said firmly. Again, Littlefoot didn't move. "Ach, ach," Phillip felt ridiculous making that noise. It was the kind of sound that would draw attention, and he hadn't heard anyone else use it.

"You're not very good at this," Xavier said. "Here, watch me."

Phillip gladly stepped aside, and the boy commanded Littlefoot to back up. The horse obeyed. "See? Now you try again."

He rubbed the back of his neck as he took his position in front of the horse again.

"I'll stand next to you and we'll do it together," Xavier said.

He nodded and stretched his arms out. Xavier did the same, and together they walked forward and commanded the horse to back up. Littlefoot obeyed this time, but Phillip was pretty sure his attention was on Xavier instead of himself.

"Good job! You did it," Xavier said, patting him hard on the back.

"Thanks." Phillip chuckled. "You're a pretty good teacher."

"Excellent job, everyone. We're going to do a few more simple commands like this one, and then you'll brush your horse and give them a reward for doing such a great job today. But before we move any further, I want to take a moment to explain what this teaches, because most people don't recognize the benefits of the group sessions when all we're doing is moving trained horses around an arena."

Several people chuckled.

"Yes, these horses are trained. But they can sense things about humans—our emotions, our mental state—and this can affect a horse's mood and state of mind and whether they will listen."

Phillip wondered what it was about him that Littlefoot didn't like. Had he sensed something was off? He was uncomfortable and discouraged by the thought. Shouldn't Littlefoot want to make him feel better?

"But these sessions aren't about training a horse, they're about releasing our fears, learning to trust, determination, confidence, and the value of hard work. When you command a twelve-hundred-pound animal to move a certain way, and it listens to you, that gives you a sense of accomplishment. It builds your confidence and gives you some determination to keep moving forward. You and your family are learning new skills that will carry over to other areas of your life.

"My job in training these horses is to make sure they don't react negatively. Ever. I know I don't have to explain to any of you how big emotions can play out, and how explosively. I train the horses not to rear, kick, or spook when that happens. But every new person who comes in contact with a horse will have a unique relationship with that animal.

"They have to learn to trust you as much as we learn to trust them. So in that sense, you really are training them, but it's not about training a horse to obey us, it's about learning to trust each other.

"Billy gave me permission to share an example from his time with us." She stepped up to a dark-haired, pimple faced teenager and wrapped her arm around his shoulders. "Billy was struggling in several subjects in school and it made him feel like he wasn't very smart and would never be smart. When he started working with Lincoln about two years ago, he thought the classes would be easy. Right, Billy?"

The boy blushed and nodded, and Heather squeezed his shoulders.

"But after a couple of lessons, he realized it wasn't as easy as he thought, because Lincoln doesn't respond well to force and Billy was a little too hard with his cues at first. He learned that working with horses involves give-and-take. He had to understand the horse, just as much as the horse had to understand him. Billy was frustrated and believed he couldn't learn to work with horses, just like he couldn't succeed in school. But we helped Billy change that thinking by showing him he needed a different approach, and once he lightened up with his cues, Lincoln started responding better. After a few weeks, Billy and his parents talked to the school to find out if they could provide him with some learning aids in class, and the school was more than willing to accommodate Billy. A couple weeks ago, Billy brought his report card to show me and it was chock full of A's and B's. He took what he'd learned here and used it to advocate for himself. And I believe—Billy, tell me if I'm wrong, but that was your idea to ask the school for the aids, right? Or was it your parents' idea?"

"Mine," he mumbled.

"Yeah, Billy moved from being a frustrated kid who got into trouble because he didn't see a way out to being almost a straight-A student. So, if you don't see the benefits these sessions can have with these simple exercises, I would encourage you to talk to some of our staff and clients, and I guarantee you'll hear many more stories like this one. It isn't an overnight change. It takes hard work and determination, but we're here to help you build up that grit for use in everyday situations. All right, next exercise…"

Phillip hung back while the horses were returned to the barn.

"I hope our son didn't make the class too overwhelming for you," the skinny blonde said.

"No, not at all. He was great."

"I'm Jan, by the way, and that's my husband Derek."

"It's nice to meet you. I'm Phillip. I'm an old friend of Scott and Heather's."

"It's pretty amazing what Heather has accomplished here," Jan said.

"Yeah, it sure looks like it."

Xavier ran out of the barn toward them. "Can we get ice cream now?" he asked, leaping and clinging to his dad and nearly bringing him to the ground.

"Careful, bud," Derek said. "You're a lot bigger than you think you are, you little monkey."

Xavier laughed. "I'm not a monkey."

"Come on, let's go," Derek said.

"To get ice cream?" Xavier asked.

"Yes, to get ice cream," Jan said, laughing, and waved at Phillip as they headed off.

Scott pulled up in his SUV, climbed out, and headed toward the barn. He hadn't seen Phillip, and Phillip didn't call out to him. Instead, he watched Heather as she said goodbye to the other class participants and thought about what she'd said during the class. Mom had pretty much admitted she feared failing Grandma again. How could he convince her there were other ways, a different approach? Was putting Grandma in a care facility the best way to go about it? Unless Richard and Denise wanted to take over, or himself, he didn't see any other way. And he couldn't see Mom being thrilled about either of those scenarios.

The last family said their goodbyes and headed to their car. As they walked off, Scott joined Heather, and seconds later, they were both headed in his direction.

"So, what did you think?" Heather asked.

"It was interesting. I can't really see my mom agreeing to come, though."

She shrugged. "That's okay. Maybe your mom needs to find someone she can talk to. I noticed Littlefoot was giving you some trouble."

He looked away, embarrassed. "Yeah, he seemed more focused on Xavier than me."

She chuckled. "Yeah, I hope you don't take it personally. Those two have a pretty special bond, and Littlefoot is stubborn, anyway."

"Seriously, man. I don't think that horse likes anyone but that kid." Scott said.

"It was fine," he fibbed. "Is Littlefoot really Xavier's horse?"

"Kind of," Heather said. "Xavier and Littlefoot arrived at my door pretty much at the same time. Xavier was a whirlwind. He was eight at the time, and his mood changed minute to minute. I had no clue how to help him. Littlefoot came to me after a traumatic accident and he wouldn't let anyone near him. During my annual fundraising event, Xavier wandered off and ended up in back with Littlefoot, which could have ended up being a dangerous situation, but Littlefoot seemed to understand Xavier was different and accepted him. They've pretty much been inseparable ever since."

"Huh. Well, he sure impressed me. You said he was only eight when you started working with him?"

"Yeah. He looks and acts a lot younger than he really is. He's twelve now, almost thirteen."

Scott shook his head. "He definitely doesn't seem ready for the teen years."

"No, or junior high, which he'll start this fall." A worried expression crossed Heather's face. "Anyway, I'm glad you came and I hope you got something out of it, even it Andi doesn't come."

"You know, the town is starting up movie night again soon," Scott said. "Maybe you can convince your mom to get out and be around people."

"That's a good idea. I bet your grandma would even love to get out for a little," Heather said.

"It can't hurt to try," Phillip said.

"Any update on your partnership with Casey?" Scott asked.

He nodded. "She sent over a contract this morning. I read it over once and it's not at all what she described to me in person, but it also looks like a standard business contract and doesn't have any details about the building on Third Street, so I need to take some time to go through it, talk to Casey about it, and see what we can change."

"How did you two even get reconnected?" Heather asked, her mood shifting from friendly to polite.

"Scott and I had coffee at the Old Place a few days after I got here. Casey was there and inserted herself into our conversation."

Heather nodded. "Sounds like Casey. Do you think you'll actually go into business with her?"

He shrugged. "I wasn't convinced I could trust her before she sent over the contract, and now that I've seen it, I'm less confident. But it gives me something to do while I'm here. I guess you could say it's a distraction from everything going on at Grandma's house."

Heather gave him a small smile. "Well, I better go make sure everything is taken care of in the barn. Have a good night."

He watched her a moment, wondering why her demeanor had changed when Casey was brought up. "Hey, Scott, do you have a minute?"

Scott glanced back at Heather. "Yeah man, what's up?"

"I need a third-party opinion." He told Scott about Jake wanting to visit him while he was in town, his reasons for not wanting to, and both his mom's and Richard's arguments as to why he should consider it. "I don't know what to do. I guess I can see my uncle's point—to do it for my mom and to let go of the pain, but … I really hate the thought of meeting with him."

"Yeah, that's rough. I mean, I remember that birthday party you had when your dad showed up drunk, got angry and knocked over the table with all the food on it before walking out. And … wasn't he arrested later that day, too?"

"Yeah, for driving under the influence."

Scott shook his head. "I totally get why you wouldn't trust the guy, and I'm sure more happened than I ever saw or heard about. But I agree with your uncle that you've got to let go of that pain and get healing for yourself. I don't think I can say if he's right about meeting with him for your mom's sake, because I don't know all the details there, but if the only person your mom is talking to right now is Jake, then maybe you talking to Jake as well will help her open up to you and be honest about what's going on with her. Plus, if you meet with him, you'll be able to see and decide for yourself if he's really changed or not. You've got the Holy Spirit to draw on now. If you're listening carefully for guidance, God's not gonna let you down."

"That's true. Thanks, man."

"Sure thing."

Chapter 16

The sounds of dishes being moved around and cupboards opening and closing brought Phillip's attention back to the present and away from Casey's contract. He'd sent her an email last night asking why she'd sent him a standard business contract. Her response had been short. Not even an explanation, just "We'll work on it together." So this morning, he'd printed it out and was going over it carefully, rewording sentences, adding new ones, and crossing out others. The way it was written left him with little else than the privilege of being the face of the company and ten percent of whatever the spa brought in. Granted, he didn't have to front any money for the project, but ten percent wasn't much.

"I'm making Grandma some lunch. Do you want anything?" asked Andi.

"Um, yeah, I could eat. Do you want help?"

"No, I was going to make her usual sandwich. I'll make two if you want one."

"That works for me. You aren't eating?" Phillip asked.

"Not hungry. What are you working on over there?"

He stretched and got up. Mom was in her robe again, her hair uncombed. "Do you remember Casey Calloway?"

"You mean the richy-rich girl from across the lake who dragged you around that one summer?"

"Yeah, her." He scratched his chin.

"I remember. What about her?" Mom grabbed the cutting board and a knife and started slicing a tomato.

"She sent me over a contract to go into business with her."

The knife paused mid-slice, and Mom looked at him. "Seriously?"

"I haven't decided if I'll accept, but I figure it can't hurt to look over the offer."

She resumed slicing but shook her head. "What kind of business does she want to start?"

"A luxury spa. You know the old building on Third Street that's been empty for a while? I guess it was the temporary library when the new one was being built."

"Oh yeah, I know which one you mean."

"That's where she wants it to be."

"A luxury spa." She spread mayo on four slices of bread, then placed the tomatoes on two of them. "I'd love a place close by to get massages, but I don't know about *luxury*. That sounds expensive."

"Knowing Casey, it will be."

Mom made a face, topped the two sandwiches with lunch meat, and placed the bread on top. She handed one to Phillip.

"Thanks. If you could choose a business to go there, what would you choose?" he asked.

She shrugged. "I'm not sure. Something that benefited the residents instead of tourists. We already have a lot of options for tourists. Even the restaurants price their food higher because tourists would rather eat up here than drive back to Ogden. What would you do if you were the one deciding?"

"I haven't given it much thought. Right now, my only concern is if it will bring in enough money so I can figure out what my next move is."

"Are the apps not working out?"

He shook his head. "Not really. The one I've been working on is a bust. My one remaining business partner bailed on me earlier this week."

"Oh, I'm sorry. It's not because you're here, is it? You don't need to sacrifice your career to be here, you know."

A twinge of pain shot through him. "I'm not. He was talking about quitting before I came. I just think it might be time to try something different."

"Well, if you're considering going into business with Casey because you think you need to stick around here, don't."

Irritation replaced the hurt he felt. "Are you trying to tell me I've overstayed my welcome?"

"No, of course not. But you seem undecided about when to go back to California, and I'm trying to assure you everything here is fine."

"Is it, though?"

She sighed. "Yes."

He nodded, unconvinced.

"Have you given any more thought to talking with your dad?" Her voice was soft, and she didn't make eye contact with him.

He hesitated. After talking with Scott and hearing what Richard had to say, he could see why it might be a good idea. But he still didn't want to. "Yeah, I have."

Mom looked up at him, a sparkle of hope in her eyes.

"I'll meet with him, but only because you want me to."

She grinned and stretched her arms across the counter to hug him. He leaned over and accepted the embrace. "I'll call him and arrange it." She released him. "This will be good for you both."

Picking up Grandma's plate, she headed for the hallway.

He shook his head and returned to the kitchen table. He glanced at the time on his phone. Richard was supposed to pick him up in a couple hours so he could return his rental car. No sense spending money on a vehicle he wasn't using very much. He ate his sandwich and finished looking over the contract. After typing up all the details, he emailed it back to her.

As he hit send, Mom returned and sat at the table. She pushed a piece of paper toward him. "Tomorrow afternoon."

He sighed. "Okay. Tomorrow it is."

She smiled, patted the side of his face, then got up.

"Mom, wait."

She stopped and turned around.

"There's a movie night at the park in a couple of days. It might be fun if we took Grandma."

She thought for a moment. "Yeah, that does sound fun. Okay."

He grinned, and she headed back to her room.

His computer pinged. Casey.

I'll look it over, but all of this is contingent on you securing the building. That's a non-negotiable for me. <3 CC

She followed that with the contact information for the current owner of the building. He didn't like the idea of doing work for her before a contract was signed, but it couldn't hurt to talk to the owner, see if he could get a read on him and find out what it would take to convince him to sell.

He opened a new email and sent a brief message to the owner, introducing himself and requesting a meeting to chat about the building.

Chapter 17

Richard tapped on the steering wheel in time to the worship song playing on the radio as he watched Phillip exit the car rental facility and head in his direction.

When Phillip climbed in and had his seatbelt on, he put the SUV in gear and headed back to Mylin Valley. "Any issues?"

"Nope."

"How are things with Andi and Grandma? I haven't checked in for a few days."

"Okay, I guess. Mom hides in her room most of the day, but makes a point of telling me that I can return to California whenever I want."

Richard shook his head. "I'm sorry, Phillip. I wish I knew what else to do, but the hospital didn't seem to think she was a danger to herself. Maybe you should start thinking about getting back to your life."

"I've agreed to talk to Jake."

He glanced at Phillip, surprised. "Really? When?"

"Tomorrow afternoon. I'm dreading it. But Mom was so happy she agreed to go to the movie night this weekend and bring Grandma."

"Well, I'll make sure your aunt and I are praying for you and that meeting tomorrow. I hope it goes well for you."

"Thanks."

They drove in silence for a while. Occasionally, Richard glanced over at Phillip, who was staring out the passenger window. He was proud of his nephew and nervous for him at the same time. He wished he could take all the pain and suffering he'd endured as a child and replace them with only happy memories.

Since he and Denise could never have children of their own, he'd always taken a keen interest in the life of his nephew. Jake was in jail when Phillip was born and wasn't released until he was about three years old. Until then, Andi had somehow made it work on her own. When Jake returned, Andi enrolled Phil in daycare, since Jake was able to contribute financially. But that only lasted about a year. By then, Phil was in preschool.

He and Denise had reached out periodically to offer their assistance, but she'd always refused. But with Jake in jail again, she needed someone to pick Phil up from preschool and watch him until she got off work. They were more than thrilled to spend time with the little guy.

As he became older, though, the routine and business of running a church took more of their life, and Phillip, although with them, had to entertain himself through various meetings and events. Now he wished he could go back and change things, make Phillip more of a priority, so he would know he was loved and valued and he wasn't alone in the world.

Maybe that's where he'd failed with the church as well. Sure, he'd given his whole life to build and lead Mylin Valley Life Church, but had he given his attention to the correct things? The people were the most valuable asset, but lately he'd been grumbling about the people, and his responsibilities weighed heavily on him.

He glanced at Phillip again. His head rested against the back of the seat, his eyes closed. Phillip had said the Sunday service at church was unique and he'd been engaged the entire time. Was it possible he'd lost focus on the people of his church, and that was the source of his discouragement? He didn't know, but he had an opportunity right now to give his full attention to his nephew. He cleared his throat, and Phillip opened his eyes and looked at him.

"You doing okay over there?"

"Yeah, I just want tomorrow to be over with."

Richard reached over and patted his arm. "What's the worst that could happen?"

"I guess I'm afraid we'll both get angry and come to blows."

"That would be bad. But I don't remember you ever getting into fights before."

"I haven't. But when it comes to Jake …"

"The anger is explosive?" Richard offered.

"Yeah, I feel like I can't contain it, and that scares me."

"So you avoid it."

Phillip nodded.

Richard hadn't ever considered this, but it made sense. Of course Phillip would wonder if there was any of his dad in him. "Then I'm extra glad you're meeting with him."

"Why?"

"So you can see that you're not the kind of man who flies off the handle, or starts fights. You can face him, talk to him, and not lose control."

"How can you be so sure?"

"Because I know you." He smiled at Phillip. "And because your aunt and I will be praying for you."

Phillip chuckled.

"It might be hard to see right now, but I really do think this will be good for you. Help you let go of some of that pain and anger you've held onto for so long."

Phillip nodded. "I hope so."

Richard hoped so, too.

They reached the house and Phillip climbed out. "Thanks again, Uncle Richard."

"Any time."

He waited until Phillip entered the house before heading home, where Denise would be waiting for him. He'd been able to put off talking to her for a few days since they'd had several meetings, both scheduled and unscheduled, to attend to. But when he'd left to run this little errand, she'd made it clear that they would be having a talk once he returned home. He knew it was time to tell her what was on his mind. He'd hoped he'd have more answers so he wouldn't make her worry too much.

When he entered the house, Denise was sitting on the couch holding a cup of tea, waiting for him. She motioned to a full mug of coffee sitting on the side table, then patted the cushion beside her. "Come tell me what's going on."

He sat, picked up the coffee mug and took a sip. It was piping hot and fresh. He set the mug down again and adjusted in his seat so he was more comfortable, then cleared his throat. "I've been discouraged lately."

Denise furrowed her brows. "Why?"

"Ever since I started to consider retirement, I've been thinking about my life as a pastor, and I feel like I've come up short."

Denise set her mug on the coffee table. "Well, of course you have." She clasped her hands in her lap and leaned forward slightly.

"Excuse me?"

"You're human, aren't you? You can't expect to have gotten everything correct."

"Well, sure. But I've missed the mark by quite a bit. Just look at my relationship with my sister."

"What about it?"

"It's terrible!"

"I don't recall the Bible saying anything about perfect, happy families in the body of Christ. You may receive the brunt of your sister's anger, but that doesn't mean it's you she's angry with. And you know that. I don't know why you're doubting it now."

He stroked his beard and stared at his wife, a growing mound of frustration rising in his chest at her strong words. He'd always known her to speak her mind, but it hadn't rankled quite like this before. "Andi's been angry for so long, and this whole suicide question makes me think I should have done something to try to help her sooner."

Denise rested a hand on his knee. "Richard, your sister hasn't been willing to receive help. Still isn't, as far as I can tell and from everything Phillip has said. All we can do is pray that she becomes willing and seize the opportunity when it does come. Your relationship with her has never been very strong. And as you know quite well, you have to have relationship in order to speak into someone's life. You founded our church on that concept. I've never seen you lay so much blame on yourself. You weren't there when everything went downhill for Andi."

"Exactly. I wasn't there. I—"

Denise held up her hand. "You were in college. And as I recall, when your father disowned Andi, you reached out to her and told her you didn't feel the same. Andi has got to deal with her anger, the same as all of us. Holding onto harmful emotions seems to be a theme in this family."

"Perhaps, but it's not just my sister that has me discouraged. We are so busy at church. People constantly ask us to do things they should be doing for themselves."

"Like what?" She picked up her tea again, but didn't take a drink.

"Like our leaders asking us how to solve simple problems we've equipped them to handle. We should have more mature Christians in our church by now."

Denise raised her eyebrows. "Says who?"

He grunted in frustration. "I do."

"So you're in charge of their spiritual growth and have placed a time limit on it, have you?"

He stood up. "Denise, I am not in the mood for this kind of lecturing. You know that's not how I feel."

"Yes, I also realize you could have asked the small group leaders if they could take over the Sunday service when Andi was in the hospital, but you didn't. As I recall, you didn't want to throw them in the deep end before they were ready.

You constantly take on tasks you could hand over to someone else. We may very well have spiritually mature leaders in our church, but you're too afraid to let them lead."

"I'm not … what would I be afraid of?" He began pacing the living room.

"Afraid to give up command of your ship? Afraid they may fail and you'll have to clean up the mess? You tell me. You've had wonderful ideas in the past four years about how to change things up, get people more engaged in their own spiritual growth, but you've been reluctant to hand over the reins."

He shook his head. "I'm going to go take a walk."

Chapter 18

The man with shoulder-length black and silver hair, wearing a leather jacket with his hands stuffed in the pockets and staring out at the lake, was instantly recognizable to Phillip. He pulled into the parking area next to one of the beach access points and considered making a U-turn and leaving. But he'd made a promise to Mom. He was doing this for her. So he parked Mom's car on the other side of his dad's restored 1971 AMC Hornet and climbed out. The one thing Jake could always be counted on for was restoring old cars.

Jake watched him from his spot on a little hill near the parking area but did not approach. Phillip considered the metaphor of taking the high ground, but then also realized the high ground was considered the best location when fighting your enemy. Either way, Jake seemed to have the upper hand, and walking up to him made him feel like the small, scared little boy who hid under the table whenever his dad came home in a drunken rage.

The figure before him had never looked physically imposing. Jake had always been tall and lean. It was the slicked-back hair, leather jacket, and ever-narrowed eyes that gave him the air of being someone you shouldn't mess with. Even now he held that same closed-off expression, and although the skin on his face and neck looked thin and frail and wrinkles made creases around his eyes and mouth, Phillip found he didn't want to get too close. He needed a barrier in case he needed to run, to get a head start.

Jake nodded once and removed a hand from his leather jacket pocket. "Son." He stretched out his hand.

The nervousness in Jake's voice took Phillip by surprise. He stuck his hand out and accepted the handshake. But he wasn't ready to call this man 'Dad,' so he simply nodded in return.

"Thanks for agreeing to this," Jake said, running a hand through his long hair and across his nose before stuffing it back into his jacket.

"Mom seemed to think it was important."

"Yeah. She told me all about your time in college. How well you did and all that, and what you're trying to do what with making your own business and stuff." His hand fumbled around in his pocket and he brought out a cigarette and placed it in his mouth, but didn't light it. "Super proud of you." He nodded and looked away. "I know I don't have a right to it, but I am." He removed the cigarette from his mouth and held it between his pointer and middle finger, then wiped at his nose again.

"Did your mom tell you I made partner at the mechanic shop I've been working at in town?"

Phillip cleared his throat. "Yeah, she mentioned something about that."

"I've been clean for a long time now. Three years. The most I've ever been clean in my adult life." He glanced at Phillip. "I know I wasn't a good dad, and I don't expect a relationship or anything like that. I just wanted to see you. See how you're doing and show you I'm trying. I'm trying to do better."

"That's … great," Phillip said. It wasn't exactly an apology, and he sensed there was still more to this visit than a little father-son catching-up session. Jake would want something from him, he was sure of it.

Jake shook his head and placed the cigarette back in his mouth, took a lighter from his pocket and lit it. "You don't want to be here."

It wasn't a question. "I have no reason to trust you yet."

Jake nodded and looked out over the lake, blowing out a plume of smoke that drifted out toward the water. "I hear you've followed in the footsteps of your uncle and grandparents and got tangled up in all that religion stuff."

"Yeah, I guess I did." He wondered where Jake was going with this, but the slight bitterness he'd heard in his voice didn't bode well.

Jake turned and looked at him. "Andi says you're not like them, though. Or at least not like your grandfather. That son-of-a—mmmm." He shook his head. "That man wanted to lock your mother away. Probably would have sent her to a … what's the place … a convent or something." His eyes narrowed further and bored into him.

Phillip broke the eye contact and waited. He hadn't known his grandfather, and while Mom had told him a few things, Jake's assessment of him was probably a little too strong.

"I'm surprised you would get into all that, knowing how your mom feels about it all. Was it some kind of rebellion? You were always a pretty good kid. It would make sense if you went to religion to rebel, seeing as she hates it so much."

"No, I didn't. I wasn't rebelling. And I don't think of it as a religion. That's a list of rules and regulations you have to follow. But I met God, and I felt His love for me." He looked at his dad then. "Love I hadn't felt from any human before."

Jake nodded slowly and blew out another puff of smoke, then looked at the cigarette in his hand. "I smoke these because it helps me feel calm." His gaze returned to Phillip's face. "Even though it's not healthy for me, and will probably kill me in the end. It's my crutch."

Phillip rubbed his face. He would not get into a debate about Christianity with Jake. He would not fall for the bait. "Is this why you wanted to talk to me? To see if you could rile me up about my beliefs?"

Jake dropped the cigarette on the ground and stepped on it. "No. I wanted to see for myself what kind of man you've turned out to be."

"Funny. Mom wanted me to meet with you to see what kind of man you were." Phillip opened his arms wide. "Well?"

Jake rubbed his thumb across the gray stubble on his chin. "I haven't decided yet. I'm hoping you've turned out to be the kind of man who will forgive his lame excuse of a father for messing up so bad, but …" He shook his head.

"But what?" Phillip asked, wanting to hear the rest of the sentence. What reason or reasons would his dad give for him being unwilling to forgive?

"In my experience, religious folks don't forgive too well. Even though the Bible tells them to."

Phillip chuckled. "I know what the Bible says. I know I should forgive you and let it go, but it's not that simple." He pointed at Jake. "You caused us pain. Both me and Mom. You let us down. She had to slave away at two jobs to keep a roof over our head, and because of it, I basically had no parents. I was alone all the time. I tried to do the right thing by Mom. Got a job as soon as I was old enough, so she wouldn't have to work so much. And every time you got out of jail and came home, you messed it all up again. Making promises you never kept. Never. Not once." Tears obscured his vision, and he turned his back on Jake to wipe them away.

Behind him, Jake cleared his throat. "I kept one promise."

Phillip half turned back toward Jake but said nothing.

"You asked me to stay away from Andi so you could go off to school. I kept that promise."

"Yeah, until what? A year ago?" He faced Jake again.

Jake shook his head. "That wasn't me. Andi called me. Your mom and I had called it quits, gotten a divorce. I knew I wasn't good for her, knew I couldn't be the man I always needed to be for her. So when you came to the shop and made me promise to stay away, I figured it was the one thing I could do. For both of you. I was struggling to stay clean but would probably fail again, anyway. I hated the way I was. Clean or drunk. If I was clean, all I wanted was a fix. It was all I could think about. I knew being clean was the right way to be. What I needed to do for Andi and you. But any little bump in the road and I couldn't handle it, so I'd go get that fix and I'd feel better. But it got to a point where it wasn't enough. The alcohol wasn't making me feel better anymore, and I didn't know what else to do other than drink more or take more drugs."

"I don't understand addiction," Phillip said. "That much I'm willing to admit. It's like you said. I recognize that the right thing is to forgive you. That's what God would want me to do, not because you've asked for it, but because it will be good for me, too. But I'm not ready to forgive you. I don't trust you. Not with me, and not with Mom."

Jake scuffed the dirt with his shoe. "Andi's not doing too well, is she?" Jake looked up at him.

Richard had told him Jake had stopped by the house when Mom was in the hospital. Had he or Denise told Jake about the hospital stay, or had they kept it from him?

"Your aunt was at the house the day I stopped by. She said she was giving Andi a break and taking care of Phyllis for her. But the last couple of times I spoke with Andi on the phone before that, she seemed … I don't know … not herself. I can't put my finger on what it was, but I was worried. When I called and she didn't answer, I was even more worried. That's why I went over there."

The genuine concern Jake seemed to have for Mom started thawing something inside Phillip, and he didn't like it. He might not trust the man, but Jake had loved his mother at one point. Mom had reminded him of that. Maybe he still did but realized he was too destructive a person to be any good to her.

"Will you at least tell me what's going on? Andi said it was all a misunderstanding but wouldn't say more."

"She says it was an accident, but she overdosed on sleeping pills."

Jake rubbed his hand over his face and swore.

"Uncle Richard and I think she has depression, but she won't admit it."

Jake shook a finger at him. "Depression. That makes sense. She said she was tired because Phyllis was up all hours of the night, but it seemed like it was more than that because she said she got the doctors to adjust the medication Phyllis was taking and she was sleeping through the night again, but your mom … she was still off. I could hear it in her voice."

Phillip watched Jake process this new information. A gnawing sense of irritation and guilt crept into his mind. He hadn't picked up on anything different with Mom, but Jake had? Were things so messed up between him and Mom that Jake was a more reliable observer than he was? Or did Jake know more than he was letting on? Maybe he had said or done something to make Mom take those pills and was covering. He hoped he hadn't just given Jake the details he needed to make things worse for Mom.

"Will you let me talk to her about it, son?" Jake asked finally.

"About her depression?"

Jake nodded. "I might be able to convince her to accept help."

"How are you going to do that? She won't even admit she has a problem."

Jake grinned, revealing crooked yellow teeth, and pointed at himself. "Because I've been there. I know what it's like to have a problem you don't want to admit to."

He didn't like this idea at all. There was no telling what Jake might say. He could make things a thousand times worse.

"Phillip, you aren't ready to forgive me, and I accept that. But let me do this one thing. Let me show you I've been working on myself. Let me do this one thing for Andi. I didn't just fail you as a dad. I failed her as a husband. Maybe this is the thing I can do to show you both that I recognize how much I screwed up and I really am sorry."

"You're asking me to trust you with her. Something I've never been able to do. Something I just told you I couldn't do."

Jake hung his head. "You're right. I guess it is asking too much."

He thought about how happy Mom had been when he agreed to come here. How she wouldn't open up and talk to him or Richard. If she was depressed, could she be looking to reconnect with Jake romantically? To try to feel something she thought was missing in her life? Or was it something else? Were they really just friends?

He weighed the options.

Tell Jake to get lost and leave Mom alone. Mom would probably be upset and things would continue on as they had since he arrived, until … until what? Until she accidentally overdosed again? Until Grandma suffered serious neglect?

Or, he could risk letting Jake speak with her. Maybe it would do some good, maybe it wouldn't.

"No." Phillip blew out a breath and closed his eyes. "Mom believes in you." He opened his eyes and found Jake searching his face. "The only reason I'm here right now is because she believes you really have changed. She won't talk to me or Uncle Richard. So if you think you can get her to admit she's struggling … then you should try. But I need to be there."

Jake squared his shoulders and nodded. "Thank you, son."

Phillip clenched his jaw. "Please. I'm begging you. Don't hurt her again."

Chapter 19

"Read that last bit again, dear," Grandma said drowsily.

Phillip glanced up at her from his spot on the couch. She was in her recliner, her head drooping forward slowly. If he waited a moment, she would probably fall asleep and he wouldn't need to reread the passage of the Bible he'd been reading aloud to her, but he did it anyway. It seemed to give Grandma comfort whenever her mind left her with a blank understanding of what was happening around her.

"A farmer went out to sow his seed. As he was scattering the seed, some fell along the path, and the birds came and ate it up."

Grandma gave a soft sigh, and he looked up at her again. Her head had fallen to her shoulder, her mouth slightly ajar.

He smiled, stretched his legs out, resting his feet on the coffee table, and opened his laptop to an online concordance and returned to his reading. Only silently this time.

Mom had been waiting for him when he returned from his meeting with Jake. "Well, how did it go?" she'd asked.

He shrugged. "Fine, I guess."

"He's different, right? Didn't I tell you?"

"Mom ... I don't know. Can we talk about this later?"

She'd looked crestfallen at his response, but he couldn't help it. The encounter with Jake had been overwhelming. He needed time to process.

Mom had disappeared into her bedroom again after lunch without eating or saying much, and the house was quiet. Grandma had asked him to read to her after Mom disappeared, and this was his first chance to process the conversation with Jake.

Back in California, he'd gotten into the habit of waking early to read his Bible and pray, because his days were so busy that if he didn't take time in the early morning, he wouldn't get a chance until right before bed. Often he would fall asleep a few minutes into his study time if he waited until the end of the day.

But here, he was enjoying the slower pace that allowed him to study at different times of the day and for as long as he pleased. There was no time limit telling him he had to quit, which meant he'd been able to dig into deep word studies of some of his favorite passages.

Richard hoped meeting with Jake would begin a healing process in him. He wasn't so sure that was the case. All the anger he'd collected in his youth had been there under the surface, ready and waiting to explode out of him. Richard had said he'd be able to prove to himself that he could control the anger, and he had to admit that, while the bitterness was there, it hadn't been as strong as he'd expected it to be when he came face to face with Jake. But he'd been working to keep it tamped down and locked away for so long that maybe he was better at doing that than he realized. He still feared he would turn out like Jake if it ever escaped. Was it possible, after all these years, that anger could still turn him into a man he didn't want to be?

He did a quick Internet search of Bible verses that talked about forgiveness. "God, I don't want to be like Jake. If forgiveness is the key to letting go of this anger, help me get to a place where I can do that."

He'd gotten into a rhythm of reading a verse, looking up a few words, and jotting down some notes, when the doorbell rang. Setting the laptop on the arm of the couch and his Bible on the cushion next to him, he was about to go answer it when Mom came out of her room and beat him to the door.

"Good afternoon, Andrea," a familiar voice said.

"Mrs. Eberly. What a surprise. What brings you by?" Mom asked.

Phillip kept his place on the couch but didn't resume his study. He didn't want to interact with the crotchety old woman if he didn't have to, but he was still curious about her reason for being here.

"I brought you a care package. I heard about your recent hospital stay and, even though I know your son is here helping you, and your brother and sister-in-law too, I wanted to bring a few things. Men can only be so much help and give so much comfort when a woman needs to rest and build up her strength."

"Wow, that's very kind of you, Mrs. Eberly. This all looks amazing."

Phillip strained his neck to see a glimpse of a large basket Mom held.

"Might I come in a while and visit with my old friend Phyllis?" Mrs. Eberly asked.

Phillip started to get up to let them both know Grandma was asleep and Mrs. Eberly should come back at another time, but he was too late.

"Of course. I'm sure she'd be happy to see you," Mom said, stepping back and opening the door wider.

Mrs. Eberly entered.

"She's sitting in the living room with Phillip."

Phillip cleared his throat and lifted his hand in greeting before resuming his seat. "Grandma nodded off a few minutes ago," he said, clearing his things from the couch so she could take a seat.

Mom took her basket to the kitchen before joining them. She stood next to Grandma and, seeing her asleep, lightly shook her shoulder.

Grandma woke with a start and blinked several times, looking at the surrounding faces. When her gaze landed on Mrs. Eberly, her eyes narrowed. "Diana?"

"Yes dearie, I've come to visit with you a little while, if you're not too tired."

"Oh, no. I'm not tired. Who is this you've brought with you? Is this Danny?"

Mrs. Eberly looked at him. "No, Phyllis, this is your grandson, Philip. My Danny is a touch older now, and his kids are in their teens."

"Oh my, yes, of course that's Phillip. My goodness, I should get my eyes checked."

Phillip met Mom's gaze and grinned. She returned the smile before turning and leaving the room.

Next to him, Mrs. Eberly gave a disapproving noise, then touched his arm. "Would you be so kind as to bring me a cup of black tea? No milk or sugar. Would you like some tea, Phyllis?"

"No, perhaps some water, please."

"Sure." Phillip got up and made his way to the kitchen, where Mom was sifting through the basket. "What did she bring you?"

"Never in my life has that woman shown me any kindness," whispered Mom. "But this basket is incredible! Homemade muffins, two kinds of jam, a loaf of homemade bread, and a container of chicken noodle soup."

Phillip filled a glass with water and set it on the counter before grabbing a coffee mug, filling it with water, and placing it in the microwave for a minute. "Wow."

"What do you think she wants?"

Phillip chuckled. "What makes you think she wants something?"

Andi cocked her head to one side and put her hand on her hip. "Mom used to play bridge with Mrs. Eberly and several old biddies. But since I moved in here three years ago, she hasn't been over once to visit with Mom." She pointed a finger at him as the microwave beeped. "She wants something.

Maybe just fodder for her gossip circle, but mark my words, she is not here just to visit." She used air quotes around the word *visit*, then returned to the basket.

Phillip grabbed a tea bag from the cupboard, put it in the water, then carefully carried the two drinks back to the living room. He set the tea on the end table by Mrs. Eberly's elbow, and the glass of water he offered to his grandmother, who took it from him with shaky hands and put it to her lips. He stayed, ready to assist if she needed it, and took the glass from her when she finished and set it on the coffee table before taking his seat again.

"Phillip, I hear you've shown an interest in possibly buying the old bank on Third Street. It's a historic building, you know."

How on earth did she know that? He'd emailed the owner requesting a meeting to talk about the building but hadn't received a response from him yet.

"Uh, yeah. I'm curious about it more than anything. I heard the owner might sell it to the right person."

"Yes, I've heard that too. If you do buy it, what will you do with it?" she asked, picking up her teacup and taking a small sip. She curled her lip after, but said nothing and returned the mug to the end table.

He bit the inside of his lip to keep from laughing and wondered if it was the tea she didn't like, or the way he'd prepared it. "I was kind of thinking about a high-end spa." He left Casey out, per their agreement that she would be a silent partner if they moved forward.

Mrs. Eberly narrowed her eyes at him. "A spa."

He nodded.

"Hmm." Her gaze seemed to bore into him for a moment, but she looked away and returned to her conversation with Phyllis. "So, dear, how have you been?"

"Oh, all right, I guess. My mind isn't as sharp as it used to be. I forget things a lot."

"You haven't been to church. But I guess that's not surprising, with Andrea here taking care of you." Mrs. Eberly glanced toward the kitchen.

"No, I suppose it has been a while since I've gone to church, although I can't remember. But this nice young man has been reading the Bible to me, and that brings me comfort."

Mrs. Eberly looked at him and nodded in approval. "He does, does he? That's good. And what have you been reading lately?" she asked, indicating his open Bible on the coffee table.

"Grandma and I were reading the parable of the sower before you arrived."

"Good. That's very good. I'm glad you have someone to read to you." She patted Phyllis on the arm, then stood. "Well, I must be going. Thank you for the tea and the visit."

"Of course, any time," Phillip said, holding back a grin as she glanced disdainfully at the mug on her way to the door. Phillip followed her and saw her out, then returned to the kitchen and grabbed a muffin from the basket.

"Well?" Mom asked, leaning against the counter as she ate a slice of bread with jam on it.

He shrugged. "I don't know. Somehow she heard about my interest in the building on Third Street, but that was all she asked about."

Mom shook her head and chewed thoughtfully. "That woman is up to something."

Chapter 20

Grandma's one-car garage was more of a storage room than somewhere to park a car. Boxes of stuff lined racks along the sides, old furniture filled a fourth of the space, and the back wall had a workbench, tools, and toolboxes. He looked around for some camping chairs and saw them tucked in the corner near the garage door.

There were five of them, in different colors. He pulled out three, dusted them off, and carried them through the house and outside to Mom's car. Returning, he found Mom pacing in the kitchen.

"I don't know if this is such a good idea," she said when he came in.

"Mom, you promised."

"I know, but Grandma can be difficult. She might not remember where she is, or try to wander off, or talk during the movie. I don't think we should take her." She held up a hand. "You should go, though. I'll stay here with Grandma."

Phillip rubbed the back of his neck. "Mom, please don't use Grandma as an excuse. I'll be there. Richard and Denise will be there. I'm pretty sure the four of us can manage Grandma."

Mom rubbed her hands together and continued to pace. This wasn't like her. It was almost as if she were afraid to leave the house. He walked up to her and grabbed her shoulders, stopping her from pacing. "Mom, what is going on?"

"Nothing, it's just not that easy to leave the house with Grandma. She can be like a toddler on a sugar high. And with all those people there …" She shook her head.

"Please, Mom, I met with Jake. That was really hard for me, but I did it. And you won't be taking care of Grandma by yourself. You need to get out occasionally, and this is an excellent opportunity."

Her shoulders sagged, and he released them. She rubbed her hands over her face. "Okay, fine. But I still think it's a bad idea."

"You go get dressed and I'll pack Grandma's bag," Phillip said.

Mom nodded and headed down the hallway to her room.

Phillip grabbed a tote bag from the kitchen closet and packed a hand towel, an extra adult diaper, baby wipes, a bottle of water, and some hand sanitizer into it. Then he grabbed one of the small blankets from the living room Grandma like to place over her lap and carried that out to the car as well. When he returned, Mom led Grandma out of her room, and for only the third time since he'd been home, Mom was fully dressed.

"You ready to go to the movies, Grandma?" he asked as they reached the front door.

"The movies? Oh, that does sound like fun. What movie are we going to see?"

"Uh, I think it's *The Wizard of Oz.*"

"Oh, I do like that movie," Grandma said.

They got her into the passenger seat of Mom's car. Mom sat in the backseat and Phillip drove the three blocks to the town center. He parked near the corner of the park, where several pop-up tents had been placed. Painted signs designated the tents as concessions. A large blow-up screen stood in the center of the park, and many chairs and blankets had already been set out to claim spots. Kids covered the playground and parents milled about, chatting and eating.

"We should sit as close to the car as possible," Mom said as they climbed out. "Just in case."

Phillip nodded and grabbed the three camp chairs from the trunk. Mom grabbed the bag and blanket from the backseat. Phillip opened Grandma's door and offered her his hand as she climbed out.

Then all three of them headed out to find a place to set up. As Phillip uncovered and opened the camp chairs, Mom held onto Grandma's arm. She placed the bag on a chair once Phillip opened it. "Do you want to sit, Mom?"

Grandma looked slightly bewildered as her gaze swept across the park, taking in all the people, and Phillip wondered if Mom might have been right. Maybe this was too much for Grandma.

"Do you want to sit?" Mom asked her again, a little louder.

"No, I think I might walk a little, see what all is going on here."

Mom gave Phillip a look that said: *See, I told you.*

"I'll walk with her. You stay here and keep an eye out for Richard and Denise," Phillip said, tucking Grandma's arm under his. "Come on, Grandma, I'll explore with you."

She patted his arm, and they set off. They walked slowly past the five booths offering various snacks and food items, then headed toward the playground. Grandma didn't speak; just observed everything around her with wide, interested eyes. They stopped at a bench near the playground and sat down. Grandma clasped her hands together and held them under her chin as she watched the kids playing.

Phillip saw Heather and Scott swinging a little boy between them by his arms. The blond-haired toddler giggled and screamed and begged for them to repeat the exercise.

"Oh-oh," Grandma cried, and put her hands to her face.

"What's wrong?"

She grinned. "I forgot how rambunctious little kids could be and how much joy they bring. I feel like I could sit here all day and watch them play." She chuckled. "The little girl on the swing nearly took a tumble, but her sweet father was there to catch her."

Phillip glanced at the swings and saw a man holding a crying little girl who was probably about five years old. He tried to imagine himself as a dad. More than anything, he wanted to be like the man holding his little girl. But the apple doesn't fall far from the tree, and he worried that despite his desire to be a good dad, his own father's poor traits would come roaring to life in him once he had his own children. He looked to the place where he'd last seen Heather and Scott and spotted them approaching. He smiled and held up a hand in greeting.

Scott swung the little boy up into his arms. "Hey, man." He stuck out his free arm and Phillip slapped the hand. Both of them closed their fists and bumped them together. The little boy made his own fist and held it out. Scott bumped it. "This is our nephew, Noah."

"Hi, Noah," Phillip said.

Noah gave him a shy grin, but held out his fist for a bump. Phillip obliged.

"Hi, Phyllis, how are you doing?" Heather asked, leaning over and resting her hands on her thighs so her head was level with Grandma's.

Grandma looked at her and blinked, probably trying to figure out how this person knew her. "I'm well, thank you."

"Do you remember the Fletchers, Grandma?" Phillip asked.

"The Fletchers? Oh yes, I remember Amy and Harry." She looked from Scott to Heather and back again.

"This is Scott and Heather, two of their kids," Phillip said.

"Oh!" She reached up and touched Noah's shoe and winked at him.

He giggled and hid his face in Scott's neck.

"And this is their first grandchild," Heather said, patting the boy's back.

"Aw, grandchildren are so wonderful. I have a grandchild, too. A boy. Phillip. He's ten years old now."

Scott and Heather both looked at him and he chuckled. "I am perpetually ten years old in her mind."

"Down, down," Noah said, and began to squirm and point to the playground.

"I'll take him over," Heather said, grabbing his hand as Scott set him on the ground.

Scott watched his sister and nephew walk away. "How did your meeting go?" he asked when they were out of earshot.

He shrugged. "Okay, I guess. It was uncomfortable, but there were a few things that surprised me. Good things … I think."

"That's awesome, dude. It's a start, right?"

"Yeah."

"Is your mom here, too?"

"Yeah, she's watching our stuff on the other side of the park."

"Cool, we're sitting over that way too."

"I'm hungry," announced Grandma, standing up.

Phillip stood as well. "Okay, well, I guess we're going to go find some food."

"Do you like pizza, Mrs. Barker?" Scott asked.

"If it's good pizza," she said.

Scott grinned. "They have the absolute best pizza over there."

Grandma smiled. "Thank you for the recommendation."

"You're welcome." He lifted his hand. "See you later."

The sun had set behind the mountains; golden rays shot out from behind the western slopes and scattered clouds glowed pink. "Pretty sunset," Phillip said.

"Yes, beautiful. A beautiful God painting."

"We should stop and ask Mom if she wants us to get her something to eat," Phillip said.

"Oh, yes, of course. But I don't want anything. I'm not hungry. I could use a restroom, though."

"Um, okay. These are the bathrooms right here. Do you need help?"

She glanced at him incredulously. "I certainly do not."

"Okay, I'll wait for you right here, then."

She looked him up and down, shook her head disapprovingly, and then disappeared into the ladies' room.

He clasped his hands behind his back and tried to spot Mom in the crowd. He knew Grandma was likely to need some assistance, but he couldn't very well enter a public bathroom full of women and check on her. Finally he spotted her, but she was staring at her phone and didn't once look around. Richard and Denise sat nearby, but they weren't looking in his direction either, and they were too far away to call to. He would just have to hope Grandma could manage herself this once.

Heather approached, carrying her nephew. "Okay, here we are. Time to go potty," Heather said in a sing-song voice.

The boy squirmed in her arms, and she set him down. He ran to the bathroom door and struggled to pull it open, but couldn't quite manage it.

Heather smiled at Phillip as she passed him and opened the door for Noah.

"Oh, wait, buddy. We have to wait in line."

Noah held his crotch and jumped around.

"Hey, I can take him into the men's room," Phillip offered.

Heather didn't look too sure about that idea and glanced at his nephew, who nodded eagerly. "Are you sure?" she asked Phillip.

"Yeah. Could you just keep an eye on my Grandma in there?" He bent his head toward the restroom.

"Oh, of course. Okay, Noah, my friend Phillip will take you to the other bathroom, okay? But when you're done, come right back here."

Noah ran to Phillip, a look of desperation in his eyes. Phillip scooped him up and went around the corner to the men's room. Opening the door, he set the boy down, who ran into a stall and didn't bother closing or locking the door.

Phillip closed the door and held it until the boy was done, then helped him wash his hands.

When they returned to the other side of the building, Heather was helping Grandma straighten her shirt, which had gotten tucked awkwardly in her pants.

"Thanks, Heather."

"No problem. Do you feel better, Noah?"

The little boy nodded and reached his hands up to her. Heather picked him up, and he rested his head on her chest and stuck his thumb in his mouth.

"Grandma, why don't I take you to sit with Mom and I'll grab food for everyone."

"Yes, some food sounds lovely," she said and started off in the wrong direction. He gently grabbed her arm and steered her in the correct direction. "This way, Grandma."

"Oh my, I got all turned around."

"It's all right."

"Noah and I will join you," Heather said.

He smiled at her and they started off.

Heather cleared her throat. "How is your venture with Casey going?"

"Okay, I guess. We're still working on a contract we both agree with, but I think we're making progress."

She nodded.

He watched her for a moment, wondering why she seemed to care so much about his business dealings with Casey, but she kept her eyes on the ground and didn't say any more until they reached their seat. In truth, he wasn't sure what to think about Casey's business idea anymore. She'd sent back his edited contract with some huge changes. She'd made it clear she wanted to tear the building down and start from scratch, but still claimed it could be done in less than a year.

"There they are," Richard said as they approached. He got up and gave his mother a hug. "How are you, Mother?"

"I suppose I'm doing well."

"Phil," Richard stuck his hand out and Phillip shook it.

"Miss Heather and young Noah. How are you doing?"

Noah hid his face and rubbed his eyes.

"Noah needs a nap before the movie starts, and I'm doing well, Pastor. I'm going to go put him down. I'll see you all later."

"Grandma is hungry … I think," he said. "And I could eat. I can grab food if anyone else wants something."

"We ate before we came," Denise said. "But I wouldn't mind some popcorn for the movie."

"Okay. Mom?"

She looked up from her phone. "What?"

"Are you hungry?"

She shook her head and hunched over her cell phone again.

He gave his uncle a questioning look.

Richard shrugged. "I'll go with you. Denise and Andi can stay here with Mom."

They headed to the concession booths, and Phillip decided on a corndog for Grandma as the least messy option and loaded nachos for himself. Richard had his large bag of popcorn before Phillip's orders were ready and they stood to the side, waiting.

"Has Mom said anything since you showed up?" Phillip asked.

Richard shook his head. "Not even hello. She got her phone out and lost herself in it."

Phillip sighed. "I met with Jake."

"Yes, I've been hoping to hear from you about it. How did it go?"

"Jake thinks he can convince her to accept help."

Richard snorted. "How?"

He shrugged. "He said he knows what it's like to know you have a problem but are too afraid to ask for help, and because of that, he thinks he can get through to her."

"What did you say?"

He looked up at the sky and blew out a breath, then looked at his uncle. "I told him he could try. I also told him I wanted to be there when he did and that he better not hurt her again.”

Richard nodded. “So, when will he speak to her?”

“I don’t know.”

“And how are you feeling about everything?”

He sighed again. “Angry.”

“About?”

“I don’t know. Just angry, like, irrationally so. I don’t know what to do about it.”

“Have you prayed?”

“Yes. I’m not hearing anything, though.”

“Give it time.”

“Speaking of time, how long should I stick around? I’ve been here two weeks already and don’t know what else to do.”

“You can go back whenever you want. Unless Andi agrees to seek help, there isn’t much anyone can do.”

“I guess I’m worried about Grandma being neglected.”

“Me too. But your aunt and I are here and can keep a close watch.”

Phillip grabbed his and Grandma’s food and they headed back to their chairs.

It was dusk now, and the movie would start soon. Grandma sat in her chair, her blanket over her lap. Nearby, the Fletcher clan sat on blankets and passed food around from a cooler.

He took his seat between Mom and Grandma and set his nachos on the ground so he could offer Grandma a bite of her corndog. Denise held out her hand.

“I’ll help her with that so you can eat.”

“Thanks.” He handed her the plate and picked up his food again.

He caught Heather glancing in his direction a couple of times, her look thoughtful … or … perhaps concerned? He didn’t know if Heather liked him as much as he did her, but the thought of being in a relationship and potentially treating a woman the way Jake had treated Mom scared him. His girlfriend in college had scared him off with all her talk about marriage and kids. But what if it was more than that? What if the very idea of marriage scared him because he was afraid of treating the woman he loved badly?

Music played, and the giant screen lit up. The crowd cheered, clapped, and then silenced.

"I'm not hungry," Grandma said, pushing the food away.

"Okay. I'll put it down here in case you change your mind."

The intro credits were still rolling when Grandma tossed her blanket from her lap and stood up.

"Phyllis, where are you going? The movie is starting," Denise said, standing as well.

Mom sighed behind him. "You better switch me places," she whispered to him.

"Are you sure? I don't mind taking care of—"

"Just move," she ordered.

He obeyed and moved to her seat.

"Mom, stay here," Andi hissed, grabbing Grandma's arm.

Grandma pulled her arm away. "I want to see the flowers."

A few heads turned to see what the commotion was.

"It's dark. There are no flowers to see. We're here to watch a movie. Now sit down."

Grandma obeyed, but folded her arms and pouted. Mom returned the blanket to her lap, then took a seat, resting her elbow on the arm of the chair, and rested her forehead in her hand.

As Dorothy tried to tell her aunt and uncle what had happened to poor Toto, Grandma sneakily reached over and grabbed a handful of popcorn from the bag Denise was holding, but did it so quickly and unexpectedly that the bag tipped and nearly half of the popcorn fell out.

Denise recovered the bag and Grandma held her prize to her chest, but didn't eat it. Instead, she threw pieces of popcorn at the people sitting in front of them.

"Mom, stop it," Andi hissed, arresting her throwing arm.

Grandma threw the remaining popcorn at Andi's face, whined, and squirmed to free herself from Andi's grasp.

Richard came over and knelt in front of her. "What is it, Mom? Do you need to go for a walk?"

More heads turned their direction. Guilt stabbed at Phillip, and he wished he could melt into his chair and disappear. He put the rest of his nachos under his chair and prepared to help the moment he could.

"No, get away from me. Don't touch me."

The Fletchers were watching now, concerned expressions on their faces.

Andi released Grandma's arm and buried her face in her hands.

"There, no one is touching you. Now what do you need, Mom?" Richard asked.

She folded her arms and twisted her torso away from him, pouting.

He sighed and stood, taking his seat again.

But as soon as he was seated, Grandma bolted up out of her chair and began walking through the crowd. They all stood at the same time. Phillip and Richard took off after her.

Several people complained about their view being blocked. Phillip apologized as he made his way through the crowd. They reached Grandma. Phillip got around in front of her, and Richard grabbed hold of her arm from behind.

She shrieked and tried to pull away.

"Grandma, we have to go back to our seats," Phillip pleaded.

"Get away from me! Help!" she shouted and reached out for a woman sitting on a blanket nearby. "They're trying to kidnap me!" she yelled.

"Okay, Mom, let's you get you out of here," Richard said, scooping Phyllis up in his arms. He carefully walked back with her to their seats.

"We aren't kidnapping her, I promise. She just has dementia. So sorry," Phillip said to the people sitting there, before following his uncle.

Harry senior, Heather, and Scott Fletcher were standing with Denise when he got back. "Are you sure there isn't anything we can do to help?" Scott asked.

"No, we're going to get her home to bed," Denise said.

Scott clasped his shoulder. "If there's anything I can do, man …"

Phillip turned away, too embarrassed to speak.

Denise wrapped her arm around his shoulders as Scott released his grip. "Andi started packing the chairs up after you and Richard went after Phyllis. I cleaned up everything else. They'll be in the car waiting."

He nodded.

"Hey, don't be discouraged. This was a good idea. Baby steps." She squeezed his shoulders and rubbed his back.

"Mom said it would be a bad idea. Now what am I supposed to do?"

Denise stopped him and forced him to turn and face her. "This isn't your problem to solve, Phillip."

"Then why am I here?"

"To be supportive."

A lump formed in his throat. He nodded, and she released him. As he walked to the car, he wiped his hand over his face. What was he supposed to be supportive of? Mom wouldn't admit there was anything wrong. And maybe there wasn't. She'd been right about this outing. Her worries had been on target. She knew Grandma better than any of them. Maybe the pills had been an accident, and now that she'd had a chance to rest, everything was fine again.

Grandma and Andi were in the car when he arrived. Richard stood nearby, waiting for him. "Do you want us to follow you to the house?"

He shook his head. "We'll be all right."

Richard pulled him into a hug. "Call if you need anything."

He nodded, then climbed into the car.

"I told you this was a bad idea," Mom said from the backseat.

He started the car, and they drove home in silence.

Chapter 21

The jar of peaches was almost empty, and it was the last one in the house. Phillip made a mental note to add it to the grocery list he'd been making on his phone as he scooped the last peach from the jar and put it into the bowl on the counter. He drank the last of the juice and tossed the jar into the recycle bin under the sink.

Opening the fridge door, he grabbed the container of whipping cream and placed a healthy dollop on top of the peaches before returning the cream to the fridge and grabbing a spoon. He took the bowl to his grandmother, who sat in the armchair in the living room.

Since the disaster at the movie night two days ago, he had found himself the sole caregiver for Grandma. Mom refused to leave her room and had locked the door. He frequently went to it, tapping on it lightly to make sure she was all right. At first, she hadn't responded, and he'd worried she'd overdosed again, but eventually she'd told him to go away. Not knowing what else to do, he decided that as long as she continued to make noise whenever he checked on her, he would leave her be.

Last night, he'd finally called his aunt and uncle to tell them what he was dealing with. Since they'd had church that morning, he knew they were busy and didn't want them to have to worry or try to make last-minute changes.

They'd agreed to stop by this afternoon. He'd just cleaned up the kitchen after lunch when Grandma asked for her favorite snack. Now he sat on the couch and watched her.

All in all, taking care of Grandma hadn't been too difficult. She had her moments when she couldn't remember who they were, or where she was, and that sent her into a frightened frenzy, but mostly she was calm and compliant. However, having to repeat yourself constantly, having to remind her who you are, and watching her slowly grow worse over time, requiring even more time and energy, would become tedious.

His phone buzzed on the coffee table, and he glanced at it. It was Scott, again. He'd sent several texts over the past two days asking how they were all doing and if he could do anything. He'd ignored the messages, including this one, got up and took the now empty bowl from Grandma and carried it to the kitchen, where he rinsed it and added it to the collection in the dishwasher.

He'd had a lot of time to reflect over the past couple of days. He'd been home two and a half weeks. But what good was he doing? Mom was locked in her bedroom, and he was caring for Grandma. Jake had promised to help, but that was five days ago and so far he'd done nothing. He shook his head and returned to the living room. Of course, he couldn't rely on Jake. He'd probably decided he couldn't help her after all. Or he had done something to hurt Mom and decided it was best to keep his distance.

"Do you need anything, Grandma?"

"Some classical music would be lovely."

On the bookshelf beside the piano, there was a small portable CD player and a box of CDs. He found one with classical piano music and popped it into the player. He waited for the music to begin and adjusted the volume.

Grandma sighed, rested her head back, and closed her eyes. "That's lovely."

Phillip resumed his seat on the couch and opened his laptop. He pulled up the email response he'd received from the owner of the old building on Third Street, Grant Porter. The man was willing to meet with him and discuss the possibility of him selling, but preferred to talk details one on one instead of over the internet. Phillip just needed to contact him to set up a day and time. But if Mom refused to come out of her room, he might not get the chance.

And what was the point of going through with all this? He needed to get back to California and start figuring out what his next move would be. Casey had sent him a revised contract, and it still wasn't good enough for him. Would it ever be? The longer Mom hid herself away, the more pointless his being here felt.

Taking over Grandma's care enabled her to stay locked up in her room. If he left …

He looked over at his grandmother. He didn't like the notion that she might have to suffer neglect before his Mom would admit she needed help, but tough love seemed to be the last option they had.

A knock sounded on the door. He got up and opened it. His aunt and uncle entered, and Denise carried in a crockpot.

"Any change with Andi?" Richard asked.

Phillip shook his head. "I knock on the door every couple of hours and tell her she needs to make some noise or I'm breaking the door down. She groans, or ruffles the blankets or throws something at the door, and I leave her alone."

"Any word from Jake?"

"No, but I haven't reached out to him, either."

"Do you have his number?" Denise asked.

"Yeah, Mom gave it to me in case I needed to get ahold of him the day we met."

"Send him a text," Richard said. "See if he responds and if he's still intending to try his methods."

He nodded, went to the living room, and picked up his phone from the coffee table. Opening his messages, he saw the one he'd ignored from Scott with an invitation for coffee if he could get away. He searched for the number his mom had sent him, then wrote a quick message.

Are you going to talk to Mom?

He considered adding more, telling him she was worse, but he decided he didn't need to know that information until he was sure Jake was still on board.

"Okay, I sent it."

"Good. Now, why don't you get out of here for a while," Richard said.

He waved the suggestion off. "I'm okay."

"No, you're not," Richard said, resting a hand on his shoulder. "You're worried and stressed, and some fresh air would do you good. Take a walk, or a drive. We'll watch after Grandma and check in on your mom."

He could see if Grant Porter could meet. It would probably be too short notice, but it wouldn't hurt to try. "Okay. If I hear from Jake, I'll text you."

Richard nodded, and Phillip grabbed the keys and headed out.

In the car, he pulled up Grant Porter's email and called the number.

"Porter speaking."

"Hi Mr. Porter, this is Phillip Hawkins. I sent you an email asking about the building on Third Street. I know it's short notice, but I had some time open up and thought I would check to see if you had some time to show me the place and talk."

"Right now?"

"Yes. If it's not a good time, I understand."

"No, no. I can meet you now. I'll see you over there in a few."

"Great. Thank you so much."

Grant Porter was a large man who wore round glasses and had slightly sagging jowls that made his ever-present frown more pronounced. Phillip recognized him. He owned the grocery store. He had to be in his late sixties, but his dark gray hair only showed slight hair loss above his temples. He always wore a three-piece suit, with a gold pocket watch chain attached to one of the buttons on his vest. And his shoes were always perfectly shined.

Being chased off the store grounds as a teenager by the man had been amusing. Having him stand in your living room with his arms crossed while he complained to your mom about your actions was not.

Amazed he hadn't recognized the man's name, Phillip felt the familiar dread of meeting Grant Porter's scowl as he watched him approach. Phillip stuck his hand out in greeting. "Mr. Porter."

"Mr. Hawkins." He gave his hand a firm squeeze as he shook it. "So you're interested in my building."

"Yes sir, I am."

"Well, let's go inside so you can take a better look. What do you want to do with the place?" he asked as he unlocked the heavy wooden door and pushed it open.

"I'm thinking about opening a luxury spa." Phillip's eyes widened as he entered. He'd seen the place, briefly, through the large, dirty windows, but he'd expected a more rundown interior. The main room was an open space, probably about 800 square feet with, four thick, round supporting columns spaced evenly. Wood paneling, in excellent condition, covered the bottom half of the walls. The top of the walls had a cream wallpaper that had yellowed in some spots but appeared to be in good condition throughout most of the downstairs. To the right of the door was a polished wood staircase with an ornately carved railing that led to the second floor.

"I should inform you that this is registered as a historic building, so if you bought the place, you'd have to adhere to the historic preservation guidelines for whatever renovations you would do."

Phillip climbed the stairs. "I understand this used to be a bank."

"That's right. One of the first banks in this area. When the larger banks moved in, this one had to close its doors as it couldn't keep up with the competition. It's been empty ever since. For a short while, it was the library, while they tore the old one down and built the new one. Built in 1885. The bank vault is still upstairs in the room on the far left. That was the bank manager's office."

The upstairs was more of a loft, about half the size of the main floor. It had two columns, the same half-walled wood paneling and wallpaper. To the right was a restroom, and at the far left, a small room with built-in bookshelves lining one of the interior walls. It was beautiful. Scott had said he didn't think it was big enough for a luxury spa, and now Phillip understood what he meant. It wasn't very big. Of course, now that he'd seen Casey's contract, he knew she meant to tear it down and build something new. He wondered if she was aware of the historic registry. Probably. He knew nothing about owning a historic building, so he'd have to look into that, but despite his lack of knowledge in that area, his desire to own such a beautiful place was increasing by the second.

He rejoined Mr. Porter on the first floor. "It's amazing. How much are you asking for it?"

"One point three million."

Phillip felt his hopes and dreams come crashing down around him. At that price, he couldn't conceive how Casey could conceive the idea worth pursuing. Not only would they have to buy the place, they'd have to restore it—or in Casey's world, tear it down and rebuild—plus buy all the equipment and hire staff. It would be years before they would recoup the cost.

"Any chance you would come down on that price?"

Mr. Porter shrugged. "Tell me, Phillip, why a spa?"

"I was trying to think of businesses that would bring more tourists in."

Mr. Porter's frowned deepened. "Tourists."

"Yeah, but I'm not totally settled on that idea. I'd be open to suggestions. Such a gorgeous building should be used for something instead of sitting around and wasting away."

"You're interested in buying, but you don't know exactly what you want to do with it?"

The look of disapproval that crossed Mr. Porter's face made him feel like a teenager in trouble again. He rubbed the back of his neck.

"An acquaintance of mine has been trying to talk me into a brick-and-mortar business recently, and they told me about this building. Until now I've done mostly internet-based business, so it's new territory for me. I'm not entirely sure it's what I want to do, but I'm in town helping my mom and grandmother, and since I have time to consider, that's what I'm doing."

Mr. Porter frowned. "Internet-based business. What does that mean, exactly?"

"I create apps and build websites for people and businesses."

Mr. Porter rubbed his chin with his pointer finger. "So you're in the business of creating businesses to sell. You create apps, and then sell them."

"Yes, and no. I still manage the apps I've created, but if I got an offer on them, I would probably sell."

His phone buzzed in his back pocket. He ignored it.

"So if I sell to you, will you do the same thing? Create a business and then sell it to the highest bidder?"

Casey wouldn't sell the business. She'd consider it a feather in her cap, another Mylin Valley property gained for the Calloway empire. But he had fully intended on having Casey buy him out at some point.

Another buzz from his phone. "Uh … I'm not sure. Like I said, I haven't quite figured out what I want to do. I might be interested in buying it and leasing it out." He shrugged. "Now that I've seen the entire building, I think it will help me figure out the next steps. Out of curiosity, why haven't you done anything with this place?"

"The store keeps me busy enough. But I always thought this would make a great little shop. Something that provided a need for locals. Something they could only get, otherwise, by driving into Ogden."

It was odd Mr. Porter was telling him of this idea when they were standing in a building he owned that could be used for exactly that purpose. But Mr. Porter was getting older. Maybe he didn't have the energy to run two businesses. The idea intrigued him, but what did people in Mylin Valley need? They had a grocery store, a handful of restaurants, a hardware store, and a gas station.

"Well, I appreciate you letting me see the place," Phillip said, reaching for his cell phone.

"If you decide you want to move forward, let me know what business idea you settle on and I'll let you know if you're the kind of person I'd be willing to sell this place to."

Phillip paused and glanced at the man. He'd thought letting him inside was a sign he was someone he'd be willing to sell to, but apparently not. Phillip gave him a half-smile and nodded before heading out the door. He didn't wait for Mr. Porter to lock the place up but went straight toward his car, checking his messages as he walked. Two from Jake.

Sorry, I got busy. I can come by tomorrow.
Can everyone be there?

Jake wanted the whole family there. He wasn't planning on a small, private conversation. This was an intervention.

Chapter 22

The following morning, Phillip anxiously wandered around the house. Jake wasn't scheduled to arrive until after lunch, and Mom still refused to leave her room. But every noise and creak made him jump, fearing Mom would come out of her room today and see everyone arriving. He wasn't sure how she would respond to all of them there, or what they were supposed to do. He'd never been part of an intervention before.

He tried to distract himself by creating yet another counteroffer for Casey. After his meeting yesterday, he'd sent her an email with the details of that meeting, including the purchase price Mr. Porter had given him. She hadn't responded yet, but he figured even she would see the cost wasn't worth it for what they wanted to do. So, even though he continued working on a counteroffer, he didn't really expect he'd have to send it over. It was something to do to pass the time until his aunt, uncle, and Jake showed up.

Of course, he also tended to Grandma and read to her from the Bible, like he'd done almost every day since he'd arrived. But he had stopped knocking on Mom's door and demanding her to make noise so he would know she was still alive. Instead, every time he went down the hall, he would stop at her door and listen. Most of the time, he didn't hear anything, and that worried him, but sometimes her blankets rustled, and once he thought he'd heard her crying. Did she know it had been three days since she last left her room?

Finally, noon arrived. Phillip made himself and Grandma some lunch, then cleaned up the kitchen. As he placed the last dish in the dishwasher, the doorbell rang. It was Richard and Denise.

"Any change?" Richard asked.

He shook his head. "Do you want anything to drink?"

Richard declined.

"A cup of tea would be great," Denise said. "But I can make it."

Phillip nodded and retreated to the living room with his uncle.

"How are you, Mom?" Richard asked Phyllis.

"Oh, we have visitors? How wonderful. I'm doing well. How are you today?"

"I'm all right. Denise is here too."

"Denise?"

"Yes, my wife."

"Oh, oh yes, of course."

"Did Jake say why he wanted us all here?" Richard asked as Denise walked in holding a mug of tea. She joined them on the couch.

"No." Speaking of Jake, he checked his watch. Jake should be here by now.

He got up and walked to the window next to the front door. Jake's car pulled up, and he was climbing out.

Phillip opened the front door and waited for him.

Jake stuffed his hands in his leather jacket pockets as he approached. "Everyone here?"

"Yes. What are we supposed to do?"

Jake passed by Phillip and entered the house, the smell of stale cigarette smoke trailing behind him. "Wait. If I can get her to come out of her room, everyone needs to tell her how worried they are and why."

Richard stood when they entered. He nodded his greeting, but said nothing.

Jake shifted nervously from one foot to the other, glancing around the room. He removed a hand from one of his pockets and ran it through his slicked-back hair, causing a strand to come loose and hang limply to the side of his face. "Everyone okay if I go in and have a talk with her alone for a few minutes?"

They all nodded.

"Is someone smoking?" Grandma asked. "I don't allow smoking in my house." She tried to turn in her armchair to see Jake, who was standing behind it.

"No, Grandma, no one is smoking."

Jake grimaced at the back of Grandma's head before making his way down the hall to Mom's room. Phillip watched him, wondering again if he'd made a mistake in asking him to help.

Jake tapped lightly on the door. "Andi, it's me. Can I come in, please?" He waited, listening, then knocked again before trying the door handle. "Andi, it's Jake. We need to talk."

The door opened. "What are you doing here?" Andi asked, sounding groggy.

Jake stood in front of the open door but didn't respond to Andi's questions. A moment later, he stepped into the room. The door closed behind them.

Richard watched his nephew intently as they waited for Jake and Andi to come out of the bedroom. Phillip paced, pausing at the end of his short route before turning his back on the hallway again, like he didn't want to miss the moment Andi's door opened.

A palpable unease filled the house. Even Phyllis, who didn't know what was going on, fidgeted in her armchair and tried to peer around the sides of it.

All of them here, in the same place. The last time they'd all been together like this was … he tried to remember. It must have been Phil's tenth birthday party. Jake had been drinking and started an argument with Richard over religion that escalated far more than it ever should have. Jake overturned the table with Phil's cake and all the food on it. That was back when they were all a lot younger, when his stances on Christianity led to him making passionate arguments over how the church should operate and he was stupid enough to imagine that arguing with someone about it would change their mind.

Somehow, Andi had convinced Jake to take a walk and cool off. But instead of walking, he'd driven off and ended up arrested. Since he'd had multiple DUI offenses, his sentence had been lengthened to a year, and once again, Phillip had been without a dad. Of course, to Phil, that wasn't a bad thing.

That was before Andi had reconciled with their mother. Before Dad died. Not long before, as he recalled. Their family was so broken. He realized the only two threads keeping them connected were his mother and Phillip. Until their mother began to need help three years ago, Phillip had been the only tie keeping them together. From the time Phil left for college, and until their mother needed care, he and Andi didn't speak very often. And when they did, it was usually because one of them needed something. A recipe, a piece of information they knew the other had, a quick happy birthday or happy holiday message. There had been no real, meaningful conversation.

He pinched the bridge of his nose and felt Denise's hand on his leg. They hadn't resumed their important conversation since he'd walked away from it. He was still smarting from her words. Afraid to let go of control. How could she think that? In the past four years, that's exactly what he'd been trying to do. Create an environment where his people could grow in faith and become mature enough to lead. But he was discouraged because he felt he'd failed. Not just in ministry, but with his family, too.

He opened his eyes and tried to smile at Denise, but it was all too heavy, and all he could muster was a slight upturn of one corner of his mouth.

A door opened and his eyes flew back to Phillip, who had stopped pacing abruptly and stared down the hallway. A moment later, Andi came into the room in a robe and slippers, her hair wild and uncombed. When she saw them all, she turned back. But Jake was there, blocking the path.

"Come on, Andi. Everyone here is worried about you and wants to help. We're all in agreement that we think you're struggling with depression. We've all seen signs of it." He glanced around the room as if to confirm that they were all in agreement. Everyone's head nodded.

"I knew something wasn't right when we would talk on the phone. I wasn't sure what it was at first, but you sounded different. Sadder. You weren't as positive and complained a lot more." Jake bent his head toward Phillip.

"You've been hiding in your room a lot," Phillip said, and cleared his throat. "You hardly eat anything." He looked at his aunt.

Denise looked at him.

He hesitated, wanting desperately to say the right thing to her. "Accident or not, you were in the hospital. We're all worried."

Andi closed her eyes and shook her head slowly. Jake gently grabbed her arms from behind and rested his head on her shoulder.

He saw Phillip clench his fists at the sight of Jake being so familiar with Andi.

"All we want is for you to go see a doctor, ask some questions. You remember how I was when I started thinking I could handle a little booze after I'd been clean a while? I would hide it. I didn't want anyone to judge me or make me feel bad about what I was doing. But eventually, I would drink more and more and I couldn't keep hiding it. I tried; people always figured it out. You always did. Now we're all here to tell you that you're not hiding it anymore. We know something is wrong, and we want you to get help."

Andi's chin trembled.

All were silent. Waiting.

"Mom, please. Can you tell us why you keep refusing help?"

Andi pulled herself away from Jake's grasp and sat on the floor near Mom's armchair, her knees to her chest, arms wrapped around them.

Richard remembered her sitting that way often when they were kids. She would sit near Mom while Dad read the scriptures. Mom would stroke her hair, and Andi would eventually fall asleep.

He cleared his throat. Right time or not, he needed to say what was on his heart. "Andi, I want to apologize to you. I wasn't a very good big brother to you after I left home. I knew it was difficult for you here, that Dad's strict rules oppressed you. I know that's why you've rejected God. And I'm sorry for making my faith a barrier between us.

"When I left home to pursue ministry, I thought I was going to change the church, so no one would have to feel the way we did, growing up."

Andi looked questioningly at him.

"I know it was worse for you at home, but Dad had expectations for me too, and I struggled to live up to them. I mean, look at this beard."

Everyone except Andi and Grandma chuckled.

"I didn't agree with all the religious stuff and wanted to make a difference. I wanted to make church better, more about relationship with God instead of a bunch of rules everyone had to follow. But I'm starting to think that all I've done is create a different version of the same thing. And I'm sorry we haven't had any kind of real relationship since we were young. I'm sorry my beliefs have hurt you."

Their mother reached her hand out, a look of sympathy on her wrinkled features, and stroked Andi's hair the way she used to. A tear dripped down Andi's face and she leaned her head against Phyllis' leg.

Chapter 23

A wave of emotions threatened to knock Phillip off his feet. Anger towards Jake, but also a sense of gratefulness that he had come and got Mom to leave her room. Fear that he'd made a mistake asking Jake to come, and fear that Mom would simply shut down and ignore their pleadings. Concern over Uncle Richard's description of what he considered his own failures. Guilt for not being here, not noticing Mom needed him.

And now he, along with the rest of his family, watched and waited to see if Andi would say anything. She'd gone to sit on the floor beside Grandma and was crying. Grandma stroked her hair and hummed quietly. He hated seeing her cry and silently willed her to speak. *Please God, let something good come out of all this.*

"I'm not sure what to say," Andi said shakily and wiped at her eyes.

Phillip grabbed a couple of tissues from the end table and handed them to her.

After she wiped her nose with one, she cleared her throat. "I know it's not normal to spend days in bed, but the way I feel … I've been feeling this way for years." Her breath came in spasms for a few seconds, and she wiped the tears from her face. "I guess I did know there was a problem, and the report from the psychologist confirmed it." She glanced at Richard, then back down at her knees, which were still pulled to her chest. "But since I moved in here, I've been busy caring for Mom and didn't stop and think much about it." She looked at Jake and gave him a small smile.

"I moved in here to care for Mom, to make up for the awful way I treated her and Dad when I was a teenager and beyond. I couldn't apologize to Dad. I was too stubborn to try to make amends before he died. But when it became clear Mom needed help, caring for her was something I could do."

She shook her head, and more tears streamed down her face. "My whole life, I've been hurting those closest to me. Mom and Dad. Richard, I've said things to you in anger many times you didn't deserve. And Phillip, I was never home enough. Never there when you needed me most."

Phillip wiped at the tears forming in his eyes. The tension melted from his body, replaced by a deep sadness. He'd suspected Mom didn't want to give up caring for Grandma out of a sense of guilt, but he had no idea she'd been holding onto so much regret. He glanced at Jake to judge his reaction to this confession. Jake stood behind Grandma's chair, one hand resting on the back of it. His gaze seemed far away, and his jaw was rigid.

"I guess my point in saying all that is, I appreciate the concern you're showing for me. But I've done all this to myself. I deserve to suffer the consequences of a lifetime of bad choices."

Phillip was instantly on his knees by her side. "No, Mom. Don't say that. You don't deserve to be miserable. You worked hard to make sure we had a roof over our head and enough food to eat. That wasn't a bad decision. You were doing what you had to do to take care of me."

Mom reached up and stroked his cheek.

"I think Grandma knows you're sorry. I believe she knew it before she started losing her memory, because we visited her after Grandpa died. Not very often, but I think she knew, Mom. And you deserve to be happy. You deserve to take care of yourself. Please, please, get some help. I hate seeing you this way. I want you to get better, to be happy."

Tears flowed freely from Richard's eyes as his sister spoke of her belief that she deserved to be miserable. He wanted to join Phillip on the floor beside her, urging her, as he did, not to believe that lie. But Jake had quietly left the house when Phillip joined his mother on the floor.

He could only imagine what must be going through the man's head, listening to Andi. In truth, if Andi had simply not chosen to run off and marry Jake, things might have turned out much better for her. One mistake was all he saw. But there was no denying that Jake had changed. He wasn't the same man he remembered. So, instead of getting on the floor with his sister and nephew, he got up quietly and followed his ex brother-in-law out of the house.

He was almost to his car when Richard stepped onto the little porch.

"Jake."

He turned quickly but didn't retrace his steps.

"I need to apologize to you as well. I was not kind to you when you came to check in on Andi. What did you say to her to get her to come out of her room?"

Jake ran a hand through his hair before stuffing it back in his jacket pocket. "I reminded her of when I was at my worst. Hoping no one would find out my secret. But everyone already knew, and they were just too afraid to say anything, because they didn't want me to lash out at them … physically or verbally." He hung his head, then raised it again. "It was time for her to confront her issues. I could take a lashing if she gave me one, and after, I could keep pushing her. It's what I needed, every time I went to jail or rehab."

Richard nodded. "Thank you. It can't have been easy for you to come and do this, with all of us here."

Jake shrugged. "I'm pretty used to people not liking me."

It was easy enough to believe. Jake had an abrasive personality, sober or not. "Are you sure you don't want to stick around? I hope you're not leaving on my account, or Phil's."

Jake shook his head. "I told Phillip I didn't need him to tell me to leave Andi alone before he left for college. I've known for a long time now that I'm not good for Andi. All I've done is make her life worse. I was happy to help today. It was my way of making small amends with my son, but I can't do much else for her. I'll just remind her of all the pain I caused her. She doesn't need that."

Richard ran a hand over his beard. "I don't know if I agree with that."

Jake chuckled. "I'm sure Phillip would."

"Maybe. But you've been talking to her for about a year. You're the one who picked up on her being off, long before the rest of us did. I wouldn't close the door completely. If you're doing as well as she seems to think you are, you might be a good source of encouragement for her."

"I appreciate you saying that." Jake turned to leave again, but stopped and faced him once more. "Do you really mean what you said in there about your faith being a barrier?"

He dropped his hand to his side and nodded. "I've been pastoring that little church for over twenty years and I haven't seen as much change as I hoped for when I started. I don't know what would happen to my people if something were to happen to me, or I was to retire. Fewer and fewer young people are attending church, and most don't want to be involved in ministry. As it currently operates, I don't see how churches are going to keep their doors open. You could say I'm questioning a lot of things currently."

"But not your belief in God?"

"No, definitely not. I've had too many close encounters with him, heard his voice too many times and felt his presence, to ever doubt his existence."

Jake nodded thoughtfully.

The door opened behind him, and Richard turned to see Phillip sticking his head out.

"Hey, Mom has agreed to go visit a doctor and to find a therapist. But she doesn't want to talk about moving Grandma into a home until she's figured out what she needs to do to get better."

"That's wonderful, Phil," Richard said.

"Great news," Jake said.

"Yeah. Thanks for coming and talking to her, Dad." He grinned and disappeared inside again.

Jake wiped his hand across his nose.

"I bet that felt good," Richard said, smiling.

Jake continued rubbing a hand across his face and, he couldn't be sure, but it almost looked like tears in Jake's eyes. "Yeah. Makes it all worth it."

Chapter 24

When Phillip walked into Old Town Coffee the next morning, he felt at ease for the first time since he arrived in Mylin Valley. As he ordered a beverage, he glanced around the room and spotted Scott in a booth in the far corner. He was staring into his coffee mug, lost in thought.

After getting his order, he headed to the table, looking around to make doubly sure Casey Calloway was nowhere in sight. He didn't want to be interrupted by her again.

"Hey, Scott."

Scott jumped and looked up at him. "Oh, hey, man."

"Sorry, didn't mean to scare you," Phillip said, taking a seat.

"It's all good. I was just thinking. Guess I got a little lost in it. How is everything? You haven't responded to my texts and calls much since the movie night."

"Yeah, sorry about that. I was … embarrassed. But things are better."

"Yeah? That's great."

"A lot better. Mom finally agreed to get some help."

Scott sat back in his seat and grinned. "That's awesome, dude! What happened?"

Phillip took a sip of his coffee. "It's kind of crazy. When I met with my dad, he asked if I would let him speak to her about her depression, and I reluctantly agreed. Yesterday we had an intervention for Mom, and Jake was there leading it.”

“What? Are you serious?”

“Yeah. My aunt and uncle were there. We told Mom we were worried about her, and she finally admitted they had diagnosed her with depression during her stay at the hospital but that she didn't want to get help because she felt like she deserved to be miserable.”

“Wow. That's intense.”

“It was. But she called the doctor last night and made an appointment, so we're finally on the right track.”

“That's great. I'm really glad. We all felt super bad at the movie night. Especially me, since I was the one who suggested it to you.”

Phillip shook his head. “I should have let you know we were are all okay.”

Scott waved a hand over his coffee mug. “It's in the past. We're good, right?”

“Yeah, we're good.”

“Sweet. So, how are you feeling about your dad after all this?”

He furrowed his brows. “Better … I think. I can see that he's trying. I still don't trust him fully. That will take time. The anger is still there, but less. The idea of forgiving him doesn't feel so impossible anymore.”

“Dude, that's awesome.” Scott held his fist up and Phillip tapped it with his own.

“I don't really know where we go from here, though.”

“What do you mean?”

Phillip took a sip of his coffee to give himself time to consider his next words. “I'm feeling better about him as a person, and Mom will most likely continue talking to him once I return to California, which still makes me nervous. But I don't especially want to call him or meet up with him regularly or try to have any kind of relationship with him.”

Scott nodded. “I don't think you have to. As long as you can figure out how to release the pain and be able to forgive him, that's enough. But …" He grinned. "I'm not an expert in this area. You should talk to Heather if you want a solid answer."

Phillip smiled. "Nah, I don't want to bother Heather with all my issues."

"Is it the bothering or the issues that's more of a concern for you? Because I can guarantee Heather doesn't mind hearing about anyone's issues right now. Especially if they're psychological in any way."

They both laughed.

"Definitely the issues," Phillip said, picking up his mug and taking another sip.

"I'm pretty sure my sister doesn't have a problem with any of your issues," Scott said, smiling.

A sense of dread filled his stomach at the thought of Scott and Heather talking about him. "How would she know what my issues are?"

Scott laughed. "Seriously?"

"What?"

"She was there."

"What do you mean?"

"Dude. When we were kids, Heather was always around. She knew what was going on at your house just as much as I did. You couldn't tell her anything that would surprise her. She was at that birthday party your dad showed up drunk to as well."

Phillip relaxed. He'd forgotten that detail. "Right. Good point." He did remember Heather hanging out with them a lot. And Scott always attended her equestrian events, often dragging him along.

"As far as brothers go, I'm the most protective of her, and I think you two would be great together."

Phillip chuckled. "Thanks, man. But there are so many reasons I shouldn't get involved with Heather."

"Like?"

"Well, I don't live here, for one."

Scott shrugged. "Addresses can change. Try again."

He smiled and shook his head. "We're not a good fit."

Scott straightened. "Why not?"

"I have daddy issues."

Scott snorted. "Which you're dealing with. And, like I said, Heather is the perfect person to work through issues with."

Phillip chuckled.

"No, seriously, think about it. She'll be supportive. If you go to therapy, she'll understand exactly what the therapist is telling you. And if you don't go to therapy, she'll be your girlfriend *and* your therapist, because there is no way you would escape helping her with the horses or her ranch."

"You make a great argument, I'll give you that. But I don't think having a girlfriend who is also your therapist sounds like a good idea."

"That might be true. But you've always held a torch for Heather and if I've been reading the signs correctly, you still do. Do you have a better reason than the two you've already given?"

Phillip sighed and tapped the side of his coffee mug.

"Oh, you do. Judging by that look, it's a doozy." Scott's teasing manner sobered, but he smiled encouragingly at Phillip.

"I share DNA with Jake, right?" He glanced at Scott, who frowned.

"Right. So?"

"So …" he said, shaking his head. "So what if I inherited his anger issues, or something else that would be equally horrible?"

"Oh, dude. I haven't been around your dad since we were kids, but you were nothing like him then, and I highly doubt you are now."

"Really? Because all I can see are the similarities."

"Such as?"

"He abandoned my mom. In the last ten years, all I do is call occasionally. Jake never made anything of himself, and even though I've been working so hard at these business deals, I can barely provide for myself, let alone anyone else, and I'm almost thirty. I should at least have a stable income by now. Maybe I'm not violent, or an addict, but similar traits are there."

"You're being too hard on yourself, man. I bet your mom would disagree with you about you abandoning her. And all that other stuff … addiction is the reason your dad never made anything of himself or kept a job, or had meaningful relationships. I know, I narrowly missed taking that path myself."

Phillip nodded and took a swig of his now room-temperature coffee.

"Look, I won't tease you about my sister anymore. But it sounds to me like the only thing holding you back in life is fear. It's not likely any one person will succeed in convincing you that you aren't like your dad. But I know Heather has the resources to point you in the right direction so you can convince yourself."

He gazed out the window. Scott was probably right. Richard was confident he wasn't like Jake; now Scott was telling him the same thing. Even Jake said he was proud of him, which had to count for something, right? But talking to Heather about it? He wasn't so sure about that.

Chapter 25

"Do I look okay?" Mom asked, walking into the kitchen, where Phillip sat at the table working on his laptop.

He looked up at her. She wore jeans and a gray t-shirt, and her hair was pulled back into a ponytail. "Yeah."

She straightened the already straight hem of her shirt and fiddled with the neck. "Not too frumpy?"

"Mom, it's a doctor's appointment. You could go in your robe and it would be fine."

She rolled her eyes. "Somehow, I don't think anyone at the doctor's office would agree with you." She grabbed her purse and car keys. "You're okay with Grandma?"

"Yep."

She nodded, then headed for the door, but paused and turned around. "You're sure this shirt isn't too wrinkly?"

"Mom!" He laughed. "You look great. Everything will be fine. You've got this. Now get out of here."

"Okay, okay, I'm going." She smiled back at him, nodded once as if telling herself she could do this, and then walked out the door.

He watched her from the window as she climbed into her car and drove off. Shaking his head, he turned his attention back to his laptop.

Casey had sent him another counteroffer. This one was better. Much better. It would give him enough upfront cash to help Mom with any medical bills related to her depression treatment.

He switched tabs on his computer and looked again at the laws regarding historic buildings in Utah. The preservation laws had a lot of requirements for maintaining and updating a registered historic building. And since the property had a preservation easement on it, it would be incredibly difficult to tear it down; that required getting a review from the Historic Landmarks Commission.

He'd told Casey about his conversation with Grant Porter and his dislike of the spa idea. But he'd kept the preservation easement to himself until he could research it further.

Casey might have some ideas on how to get around the easement, but he wanted to understand the laws to make certain she wouldn't put him in a position where he was breaking them. It wouldn't surprise him at all if she intended to use him in that way.

He reached for his cell phone to call her, but hesitated. Ever since he'd seen the building, he'd had doubts about tearing it down. If Casey got her way, he would be agreeing to the destruction of that beautiful building and irritating the locals.

But they didn't have to put a spa there. Everyone he'd spoken with seemed to prefer something that benefited the residents in the valley rather than the tourists. An idea had been growing in his mind over the past few days that might serve both. But he was pretty confident Casey would never hear him out.

He thought about Scott's advice from earlier. Had he agreed to work with Casey from a fear he couldn't create a business on his own? He'd given up on the app for that reason, and he didn't know what he would do once he returned to California, knowing his ex–business partner and roommate would more than likely be moving out once he got hitched. He would have to find his own place. *Addresses can change.*

He picked up his cell phone and dialed the number.

"Phillip, I was beginning to think you were ghosting me."

He rolled his eyes. "Nope, I just don't like to rush into things."

"Well, since it's been a while since you called instead of texted or emailed, I'm assuming you have something important to say to me."

"Yeah, I know I told you what Mr. Porter's price tag was, but he also told me there's a preservation easement, and, looking at the laws regarding preservation … I'm not sure you'll be able to tear this building down easily."

She swore. "Of course they would try to protect that ugly eyesore. I can't say I'm surprised, but I'm positive I can find a workaround."

"What if we didn't tear the building down and did something different with the place?"

"Like what?"

"Well, I know there are a lot of farms and artisan crafters in the valley. What if we opened a small retail shop and offered to sell their wares on consignment? It would benefit locals *and* tourists."

Casey laughed. "Consignment? Oh really, Phillip. I thought you had a better head on your shoulders than that. Consignment is a waste of time and money. You'll never be good at business if you let the emotions of people get the better of you. A spa is great for tourists, but it's also accessible to the locals. The building as it stands now is too small to work. It has to come down. I'll work on finding a loophole you can use, but if you can't secure the building and get a signed contract, then this deal is off."

He sighed. "Got it."

He hung up with Casey, feeling deflated. Somewhere along the line, he'd gotten his hopes up that this deal would work somehow, but the further into it he got, the less he liked how Casey operated. Sure, he would receive a tidy sum of money to help Mom with whatever she needed and have time to figure out what his next move would be. But no one in town wanted her spa. If he was going to be the face of the company, he didn't want the whole town hating him. With most of the valley being farmers or wealthy families who'd been here for generations, he'd grown up feeling like he didn't belong. Now he had an opportunity to bring business to the town, and the whole town would hate him for it. Whether he belonged or not, they wouldn't want him here.

He furrowed his brow. Why did he care? Wasn't he planning to return to California, anyway?

His computer pinged: a new email. He switched tabs and saw it was from Richard.

Dear church leaders,

I have been doing a lot of thinking lately about the future of our church. It has always been my goal to have a congregation that encourages spiritual growth, but I've recently come to realize that in some ways I have failed in that mission. It has recently been suggested to me that I have hindered the growth of some due to my own fear of letting go of control. I've also come to the conclusion that I've been focusing on the wrong things as of late. Instead of making relationships a priority, as I've always preached, I've been focused on tasks. These have been hard pills to swallow, but as I've considered it and prayed about it, I realize both of these accusations against me are true.

Over the next few weeks, I will reach out to you individually to find out what effects my fear has had. As difficult as the conversation might be, I hope you will be honest with me.

In addition, it seems fewer young folk are interested in coming to church, and we need to figure out why that is. What are we doing, what are we saying, what are we teaching, that makes them stay away? Perhaps the answer can be found as I seek to understand my role in the way things currently stand. These are questions I cannot solve on my own, nor do I believe it is my responsibility to. We are called, as the body of Christ, to reach the lost and hurting. All of us. Not just pastors, not just as leaders in the church. All who believe in Christ and call on his name are called to love one another and show God's love to our neighbors and families.

These matters have been weighing heavily on my shoulders for some time now. I hope I have not created a church full of people who fear their pastor. Instead, I hope there is enough of Christ's love in all of us that we can be open, honest, and authentic with each other in this next stage of growth.

Pastor Richard Barker

He remembered the question Richard had asked him not long after he arrived, about problems in the church. And what he'd said to Mom during the intervention about his faith being a barrier in their relationship.

Phillip had certainly felt a barrier between himself and Mom after he accepted Christ. They never spoke of it, but any time Mom came into the room while he read his Bible to Grandma, there was tension.

The church had a long history of making people feel unworthy. It seemed to him that the cycle had to be broken, had to change. More people needed to understand that being a Christian wasn't about following a bunch of rules, but a relationship. Sure, there needed to be boundaries, and the Bible talked about certain actions being sin, but there were so many things Christians argued about with each other that simply didn't matter. If God could accept us into his kingdom exactly the way we were and then lovingly and patiently help us grow into the people he wants us to be, then we should be able to do the same.

He wondered why Richard had included him in the email. He wasn't a leader at Mylin Valley Life Church. Didn't even live here. Beyond his family and the Fletchers, he didn't have relationships with anyone in town. And those he did have weren't deep. If he returned to California, they would probably continue as they were now. Unless this business idea went forward. The money he made from it would help his family. But would Scott and Heather still speak to him? They'd both made it clear they didn't like the idea. Was it enough that he could help Mom? Or should he consider the community at large as well?

A few hours later, Mom returned, looking exhausted.

"How was it?" he asked.

She shrugged. "The doctor gave me some medication to try." She held up a small paper bag from the pharmacy. "And had me talk to a therapist so I could get an idea of what therapy would look like. The therapist was nice and explained things really well, so I scheduled an appointment with her for early next week."

"That's great! You know, Heather Fletcher does horse therapy."

She shook her head. "I don't think I want to see a therapist in the valley, especially not someone I know. I kind of like the idea of anonymity."

After his recent conversation with Scott, he understood her position. "Makes sense. Did the doctor say how long before you should notice a difference with the medication?"

"It could take several weeks. I'm supposed to take them daily and consistently. I'm worried about side effects." She set the bag and her purse on the table. "I don't know if I can do this, Phillip."

"What do you mean?"

"The doctor said the first few days after I start taking the medication could make me feel worse before I feel better, and there are all these side effects." She handed him a piece of paper with a list of potential issues that filled half a page. "I could have trouble sleeping, or headaches, blurred vision … I'm already struggling, and for this to take weeks to work … I don't know how I'm going to get through this. What if the cure is worse than the ailment?"

"I can stay and help."

She cocked her head to one side. "For how long? You have a life in California. Eventually, you need to get back to it."

"Not really."

She furrowed her brow. "What?"

"I mean, I have an apartment with two roommates, and I can get work pretty easily building websites for people. But all my business dealings have fallen through. My business partners both quit on me, and since one is my roommate, too, I suspect we'll be giving up the apartment soon, since he is talking about proposing to his girlfriend. I guess my point is, I don't know what my next move is yet, and I have time to figure it out. I can build websites from anywhere. Even here. There's no rush, and I don't mind being here and helping you care for Grandma."

"Even if I get really moody because of these pills?"

He smiled. "It can't be as bad as Jake's mood swings used to be."

Mom laughed. "You have a point there."

She opened the bag on the table, pulled out a pill bottle, and read the label. Taking a deep breath, she opened the bottle and shook one of the small pills into her open palm, then closed the bottle and set it on the table. "Well, bottoms up." She tipped her head back and dropped the pill into her mouth and swallowed it without water. "No going back now."

Chapter 26

The familiar whoosh-thump of the church's front door opening and closing reached Richard in his office, and he glanced at the screen to his left that showed the security camera footage around the building. "Hmm …" He stroked his beard as he watched his sister make her way nervously down the hall toward his office.

He saved the document he was working on, his sermon for Sunday, and put his computer to sleep. Whatever Andi wanted, it would probably take all of his mental energy and attention.

A moment later, Andi knocked on his door and he invited her in. "This is a surprise. Is everything all right?" he asked.

She nodded and took a seat in the chair across from him. "I need to apologize to you."

Richard sat back in his chair. "For what?"

"I've mistreated you for years, and you haven't deserved it."

He chuckled. "I'm sure I've deserved some of it."

Andi shrugged, but didn't smile. "Maybe, but after hearing what you said at Mom's house about your own rebellion against Dad and how you wanted to change things, it's really got me to thinking about how I've treated you over the years. I didn't know all that stuff. I always figured church had tried to catch up with the times and you were just the next generation of Dad. It was an assumption, and I realize that now. I've never tried to understand, and I'm sorry."

He nodded. "Thank you, Andi. That means a lot."

"I also want you to know that I believe the reason Phillip hasn't become like Dad is because of the influence you and Denise have had on him. And for that I'm thankful."

A lump formed in his throat, and for a moment he couldn't speak, so he simply nodded. These comments had come so unexpectedly, out of left field. All this time he'd been trying to figure out how to make amends with his sister, and here she was, coming to him. *Thank you God.* The bulk of the weight he'd been carrying on his shoulders the past few months lifted.

"I'm sure Phillip has already told you, but I've talked to my doctor and started taking medication to treat depression."

"That's wonderful, Andi. I hadn't heard that yet." He wiped at the tears forming in his eyes. "Have you talked to Jake since we were all at your house?"

She shook her head. "I was disappointed that he left without saying goodbye. I've wanted to call him. I'm just not sure how Phillip feels about it after everything, and I don't want to upset him again."

He nodded. "I think he's had a change of heart toward his dad. I know I have."

Andi's eyebrows shot up. "Really?"

"Yeah." He stroked his beard. "I followed him out when he left. He played the usual tough guy, but hearing you talk about your struggles was hard on him. He left because he's afraid he'll be a negative reminder for you as you get treatment. But I suggested that might not really be the case, and he could offer you quite a bit of encouragement."

Andi reached across his desk and squeezed his arm. "Thank you."

Richard smiled. "Phillip came to tell us you had agreed to see a doctor, and he thanked Jake. Even called him Dad. Nearly brought Jake to tears."

Andi grinned and tears glistened in her own eyes.

"You were right," he said. "I'd closed the door on Jake. Never thought he would come through for you or Phil. I guess I forgot miracles can happen." He got up from his seat and rounded the desk. As he did, Andi stood, and they hugged each other tightly.

A sharp knock sounded on his office door. He gave Andi one last squeeze before releasing her to see who stood at his open door.

It was Mrs. Eberly. "Diana."

"I need to speak with you, Pastor." She held up a piece of paper, on which he recognized the email he'd sent out to his church leaders.

"All right. Give me a moment to finish up here and I'll be right with you."

Diana nodded and retreated out of the doorway a few steps and turned her back on them, as though she didn't intend to listen to every word that left their mouths.

Richard shook his head and Andi tried to hide a mischievous smile, but failed.

"I guess I should get going," she said, gathering her things. But instead of moving to the door, she motioned for Richard to follow her to the back corner of his office.

"I wanted to tell you one last thing," she said in a low voice and glanced toward the door.

He waited.

"I asked my doctor and a therapist she had me meet for their opinion on my taking care of Mom while I get treatment. They both agree that I should focus on my own healing for a while. I still don't like the idea of putting her in a home, but I can see the benefits of it. At least for now."

Richard nodded. "I never meant to make you feel I was taking her care away from you. But I also think it's for the best. Why don't we look for a place together?"

"I would like that. Thank you. I guess I'll let you get to your next impromptu meeting."

Richard smiled. "I'm glad you stopped by, Andi."

"Me too."

"Diana, you can come in now."

She entered his office and sat in the seat Andi had vacated and waved the piece of paper above her head. "What's the meaning of this?" She set it on the desk in front of him and stabbed it with her finger before sliding it toward him.

It surprised him she had a copy, as she wasn't a leader, but it also surprised him that it had taken Mrs. Eberly this long to approach him about it. "What exactly is your complaint?"

"For starters, you're thinking of making more changes. What are they?" She perched herself on the edge of the chair opposite from him and waited.

He sat back in his chair and stroked his beard. "I'm not sure yet. I've started meeting with the leaders, but I want to see what everyone has to say before I decide what to do."

She threw her hands in the air. "You're the pastor. It's your job to lead the sheep. And what's all this nonsense about giving up control? This church is yours to control and to lead. If you don't, you'll be letting chaos run wild. You can't let yourself appear weak in the eyes of the congregation or the next thing you know, we'll have tattooed and pierced hooligans leading worship, and church will look more like a rave."

Sitting forward again, he rested his arms on top of the desk and chuckled. "Mrs. Eberly, for some time now I've been thinking about the way we do church. Why do we do the things we do in the way we do them? We've become ritualistic in a lot of ways here at Mylin Life Church. I want to change that. Being a Christ follower isn't about following rituals and rules, or appearing stronger than our fellow Christians. It's about having a relationship. I don't want to be an imposing figure that my people fear. I want to be humble and honest. To show them I'm a human who makes mistakes just like they do and as long as we're all willing to work through our issues, we can do just that.

Many people know living for Christ is about having a relationship, but they don't always live it to the best of their ability. You're right; it is my job to shepherd, to lead them to Christ. But for a long time now, I've felt like I've been bringing the sheep into the church to feed on some good quality hay, only to have them leave it at the altar when they leave instead of taking it with them. Does that make sense?"

She was silent for a moment. "You're questioning your legacy."

"In a manner, yes, I suppose I am. When I became pastor here, my passion was to help folks know Jesus the way I'd gotten to know him. Personally, intimately. And somewhere along the line, I think I became complacent and our church became like every other church, where people rely on the leaders to hear from God for them and feel they have to behave a certain way for God to accept them."

"But we do have to behave a certain way. We can't go about sinning like the world and expect God to be pleased with us," Mrs. Eberly said.

"I know that. I'm not giving anyone a license to sin here." He indicated his email. "But I do hope that by giving the leaders an opportunity to tell me, openly and honestly, if I've squashed their authority or made them feel they can't follow God's plan for their life, then good changes will come. In the Old Testament, when Moses and the people were wandering through the desert, Moses was given wise advice. He was instructed to assign leaders over groups, so he wasn't taking on the entire load himself. I've attempted to do that, but no one wants to step up. Kids' ministry is always lacking volunteers, events are always short-staffed, and everyone is always coming to me with questions about little details that their appointed leaders should be able to answer for them. What if the reason we can't keep volunteers in church is because what we're doing, and have been doing, for decades, isn't working anymore? What if the leaders feel they don't have enough freedom to take their area of expertise in the church and use it the way God would have them to, because I've placed limits on them they don't need? We need new ideas, new ways of doing and looking at things. A fresh perspective."

"It was wise advice Moses received," Mrs. Eberly said. "We need to focus on the men in the church. They are the ones who are lacking. They need to step up and be leaders in their own homes again. Women have taken on roles God never meant them to because the men are weak. You need to be firmer with the men in this church. Correct them. Admonish them. But don't give this building over to become a place where bingo is played every Saturday and various clubs take over all the rooms. This is a holy building. It's supposed to be set apart for God and should be kept as such."

"Mrs. Eberly, do you still hold a Bible study in your home?"

"Yes, of course I do."

"Well, would you say your living room is holy during that time?"

"My living room? Goodness gracious, no. The time we spend together is holy because where two or more are gathered, Christ is there in the midst."

Richard nodded and tried to hide the grin creeping over his face. "I believe wherever Christ is, is holy. But you provide individuals with an opportunity to develop a relationship with Jesus outside these four walls. We need more of that, in and out of the church. We need the church to be the church outside this building. The way things are, we limit what people can do to accomplish that. Everyone has a life to live. These days, we humans are very busy. We have a lot of stuff on our plate. What if we allow people to create an atmosphere that fits in with their lives? If we open up our classrooms to teachers who want to tutor their students after school, it could open up a way for those teachers to introduce Christ to those students. If we let the kids' soccer league use the grass outside and host a place for the league to play, then parents might sign their kids up, and find people to share Christ with. Do you see where I'm going with this?"

Mrs. Eberly gathered her bag and stood, glaring disapprovingly at him. "You'll regret this, Pastor. If you open the church up to whoever wants to use it, you'll have lost sheep eating the neighbors' azaleas!" She turned on her heel and stormed out.

Richard relaxed into his chair and laughed, a weight lifting from his shoulders. If he could irritate Mrs. Eberly so badly with his idea, then maybe … just maybe … he was on the right track.

Chapter 27

The house was quiet. Mom was at her first therapy appointment and Grandma napped in her room. Phillip took advantage of the time and used it to pray. For Mom and her appointment, for wisdom on the business deal, for his uncle, and whether he should move back home permanently, and again, for being willing to forgive his dad.

When he finished praying, he sat in the stillness and listened with eyes closed. The clock on the wall ticked rhythmically, but no voice spoke to him. Which wasn't a surprise. Typically, when he prayed about something, a sense of peace settled on him for one direction over another. Any worry or stress lifted when he considered one path over another.

He went through his prayer subjects in his mind again. Mom would be okay in the long run. The business deal was still uneasy on all sides, and he sighed. Ideally, he'd like to buy the building himself and not deal with Casey ever again. Give the place a little updating and a good scrubbing inside and out and make it into a consignment shop. But he couldn't afford one point three million dollars. Couldn't afford even half of that.

Jake's intervention and the resulting help Mom had gotten had lessened his anger toward Jake. The ice around his heart had begun to melt. Maybe he could stop asking God to help him reach the place of wanting to forgive. Maybe he was ready.

Phillip heard Mom's car pull into the driveway. He closed his Bible, set it on the coffee table, and waited for Mom to enter the house.

When she did, she was holding a couple of plastic bags and smiling.

"How was it?" he asked.

She nodded. "It was good. And I'm feeling good. There wasn't a lot to it today. It was mostly a get-to-know-you session, but like … she wanted to hear as much of my history as I was willing to share. I didn't go too deeply into things, but even sharing the little I did felt good."

"That's great."

"Yeah." She set the bags on the kitchen table. "I'm going to go check on Grandma, then take care of a few things in my room."

He nodded, disappointed that she was planning to hide in her room again. But he couldn't expect changes overnight. The fact she was taking the medication, and that she seemed encouraged by the therapy session, was a win. He could celebrate that at least.

Once she left the room, he tried to regain the sense of worshipful calm he'd had before her arrival and reminded himself that he had peace about Mom. She would be okay. It might take some time, but it would all work out.

He thought about Richard. His uncle had been preoccupied with where the church was going since he'd been there and probably much longer. Was Richard overthinking matters? Was he simply disappointed with what he'd expected his legacy to look like as he reached an age where he wanted to slow down and rest? Or had he lost focus like he said?

Phillip had a church he attended regularly back in California. It was a megachurch, though, and he'd never spoken with any of the pastors one-on-one. In fact, most members of the church he had seen speaking with the pastors had acted as though they were meeting a celebrity. That always rubbed him the wrong way, but he wasn't entirely sure that was wrong. After all, that's how people treated Jesus.

He considered this more. Most of the crowds followed Jesus and listened to his teaching, but did they really become his followers? There were the twelve, of course, and the Bible mentioned five hundred believers who saw him after his resurrection from the dead. It's doubtful all five hundred of those people got to speak with him one-on-one, and those who did were probably pretty excited about it. Heck, he'd be really excited about that. The only difference was, pastors are human. He wondered how the pastors of his church in California felt about all the fanfare they received. If he were in their position he could imagine it would be a difficult role to be in; for many reasons.

Mom returned carrying a large, and apparently heavy, box. He got up to assist, but she reached the kitchen table before he reached her.

"What's this?"

"My sewing machine." She grinned at him.

"You're going to start sewing again?"

She shrugged. "The therapist asked me to remember things I used to enjoy doing. On the way home, I remembered our conversation about your baby clothes and stopped by the fabric store." She indicated the bags.

"That's fantastic. What are you going to make?"

"I figured I'd start with something simple to get my feet wet and try a couple of baby blankets. I can always donate them to the NICU at the hospital."

"Mom …" He stared at her, not sure what else to say. So he leaned over and hugged her.

"Oh, my boy." She pulled away from him and looked up at him. "I really had you worried, didn't I?"

A lump formed in his throat, and he nodded.

Mom reached up and touched his face. "I'm so sorry."

"It's okay. You're getting the help you need now, and it's going to get better."

She nodded. "Yes, I think it just might. Now, help me figure out which of these fabrics I should start with."

From one bag, she pulled out a solid dark blue fabric, followed by a lighter blue print with stars and spaceships. From the other, she pulled out a solid red fabric, lace trimming, and another red fabric dotted with little white hearts. "I thought about putting lace around the edges of both, but now I'm not sure it really goes with the blue. What do you think?"

He agreed with her assessment. "You should start with the blue one."

She made a face. "But I got the lace to cover up any mistakes I make."

He laughed. "Okay, start with the red, then."

Mom grinned and nodded, then pulled the cover off the sewing machine and started fiddling with it.

He sat down in the chair beside her and watched.

"Mom, does it make you uncomfortable knowing I'm a Christian?"

She paused in her tinkering and looked at him.

"I was worried. Worried you would become like your grandpa. But I haven't seen that happen, and I know your childhood wasn't the best." She handed him the plug for the sewing machine. "Will you plug that in for me?"

He obliged and wondered if talking about this subject now was too soon for her. Should he wait until she was further down the road in her treatment for depression?

"I know that church and religion can bring comfort to people. I guess after a while I assumed you picked up Christianity because your childhood wasn't very good. You could find comfort in believing in God."

"There is a comfort in it, but it doesn't really come from going to church, although there is an element of that. There is more peace in my study and prayer time. I feel like God really hears me and directs me, and with all the craziness of life, I'm glad to have someone I can talk to who knows more than me, loves me no matter what I do or how I act, and guides me. I try not to be judgmental, but I know I failed with Dad."

"It wasn't easy for me to believe him at first, either." She glanced at him, then placed a spool of thread on the top of the machine, unwound a little of it and wove it through the machine. "I also didn't know you'd made him promise to stay away from me." She arched an eyebrow at him and he looked away.

"Yeah. You know how undecided I was about leaving for college."

"Yes, I remember."

"Well, I was afraid Dad would return and hurt you, or worse, convince you to get back together."

Mom chuckled. "I did love Jake at one time. But I also learned my lesson. In fact, I learned it long before we got divorced. The only reason I stayed with him is because I was afraid God would be upset with me if I divorced him."

"What? Really?"

She nodded. "I probably would have called it quits after the second time he was arrested, when I was pregnant with you. But the church I grew up in said it was a sin to get a divorce." She shook her head. "I spent so many years rebelling against so many things that the church called sin." She glanced at him. "So, so many things. The music I listened to, the clothes and makeup I wore, the people I had as friends … they were all a slap in the face with the expectations my parents had for me as a good Christian girl. And yet that one thing stuck in my brain."

"Wow, I had no idea."

She sighed. "I still have a lot of pent-up anger about the way I was treated in that church. I'm sorry if I made you think I was ever angry about your decision." She cocked her head to one side. "Although, I guess after you first told me, I was pretty angry. But once I realized you were still you, and weren't morphing into a control freak, I was okay with it."

He chuckled.

"Okay, I think we're all set up." She tested the pedal and the sewing machine came to life. "Time to test it on some fabric." She got up from her seat to grab the scissors from a drawer in the kitchen. Returning, she cut a small square off the blue fabric and positioned it on the machine. Setting it for a certain stitch, she pressed the pedal and guided the fabric through. On the other side, a perfectly straight line of neat stitches emerged. She beamed and turned off the machine. "It still works!"

She got up from her seat again and took the two bundles of red cloth into the living room. Phillip stayed where he was and said a silent prayer that Mom would come to know Jesus personally. His heart ached at what she must have gone through with her parents. He also better understood Richard's struggle. What did need to change in the church? What needed to happen in order for the world to see them as light? He shook his head, stood, and joined Mom in the living room.

Mom had laid out the solid red fabric and was measuring it. He waited until she'd finished making her marks, then said, "How would you feel if I moved back to Mylin Valley?"

She looked up at him. "Really? I would love that. Are you seriously considering it?"

He nodded.

"Why?" She sat back on her knees.

"Since I've been here, I've realized how much I've missed you, and Richard and Denise. And it was always my plan to come back once I graduated and became a successful businessman so I could make sure you were well cared for. I just haven't yet, because … well, I'm not successful yet. And … probably because I wasn't sure I'd ever belonged here."

"Successful? Phillip, there is more to life than making money. And more to caring for someone than making sure they're financially stable."

"I know. But I always hated that you had to work so much. I want to make sure you're never in that position again."

"Is this why you want to go into business with that Calloway girl?"

He nodded.

"Don't do it just to provide for me. It's not worth it. Go into business because it's something you really want to do. Okay?"

"Okay."

"Promise me."

"I promise." And when he said it, a sense of peace settled over him. He didn't know what his next move would be, and that scared him more than he wanted to admit. But he had peace about not doing business with Casey. Now all he needed was to figure out how to overcome this debilitating fear.

Chapter 28

Phillip parked Mom's car in front of the little white house where Scott's grandparents lived, or used to. He still wasn't sure.

Climbing out, he scanned the fields. He'd decided to take Scott's advice and talk to Heather about his fear of turning out like his dad. If Mom could get the help she needed, so could he. And since he was now seriously considering a permanent stay in Mylin Valley, he hoped the conversation might give him a clue about her feelings for him. Dating still didn't seem like a good choice, but if fear was really holding him back from living his life to the fullest, who knows what might happen if he overcame that fear?

Her Thursday group would begin in about an hour, and he hoped to find her in the barn. He headed toward the open barn door and peered inside. "Hello?" he said, loudly enough to reach across the barn. A couple of horses studied him from their stalls, but he didn't see anyone.

A door in the back opened, and Heather stepped out. "Phillip? Hi. Are you here for the group meeting?"

"No. I was hoping you'd have a few minutes to talk."

"Oh, yeah." She headed his direction.

"Are you sure? I don't want to interrupt if you're preparing."

"No, it's fine. I was just going through emails. What's up?"

"Scott suggested I talk to you about …" He hesitated and reminded himself his issues wouldn't surprise her. He rubbed the back of his neck. "Uh, well, about being my dad's kid." This would be harder than he expected. Mom's comment about talking to a stranger instead of someone she knew came back to him. Why hadn't he taken that same advice?

She gave him a questioning smile. "What issue is that?"

He stuffed his hands in his pockets and stared at the cement floor. "I see some of his negative traits in myself, and I don't like it." He glanced up at her.

She had her arms folded, her head tilted slightly, and she regarded him thoughtfully.

"Scott says I'm overthinking things," he added, to fill the silence.

"What traits?" she asked finally and shifted her weight from one foot to the other. Her shoulders were hunched now, and she appeared a little uncomfortable.

He was regretting his decision to talk to her. It was all-around awkward. Scott had clearly made a mistake in thinking Heather wanted to help him.

"Uh, well, we both abandoned my mom, for starters."

Heather's brow furrowed. "When did you abandon Andi?"

"When I left for college. I haven't been back since, not even for the holidays."

"My brother is right. You're overthinking it."

He waited for her to say more, but she just stood there looking at him. "Any advice on what to do about it?" he asked in a slightly irritated tone.

She dropped her hands to her side and walked past him out into the sunshine. He turned and followed her.

"What exactly are you looking for here?" she asked.

"Advice. Scott was certain you would want to help."

"Well, okay. I do want to help, but I need more information, and you're not being very forthcoming."

"What do you mean? I told you what my issue is."

"Not really."

"Come on, Heather. You know what my dad was like; how he treated me and my mom."

"Yes, I do."

"You don't see any similarities between us?"

She shook her head. "No, I don't. What is it you think I should see?"

He rubbed the back of his neck. "Nothing. Never mind, this was a bad idea." He headed for Mom's car.

"Phillip, wait. I can't help if you don't tell me what the problem is. The real problem." She blocked his path. "All you've told me so far is you think you and your dad both abandoned your mom. I told you I disagreed with you about that. Why are you upset?"

"Because you're being weird."

She pointed at herself. "How am I being weird?"

"I don't know. You were talkative and friendly at the beach, but since then, quiet and weird."

She drew in a deep breath and slowly let it out while pacing a few steps away from him. She turned toward him again and returned to the spot she'd left. "Okay, fine. Maybe I have been a little quiet around you lately." She twisted the end of her braid around her finger. "Do you remember what Scott said at the lake … the warning he gave you about how I psychoanalyze people?"

"Vaguely. I'm pretty sure he was joking."

She scrunched her nose and stared at the ground. "He said it as a joke, but it's not too far from the truth." She looked up at him again.

"So you do think there's something wrong with me?"

She chuckled. "No. But …" She trailed off and kicked at the dirt. "I may have partially diagnosed you," she said finally.

"Diagnosed me? With what?"

She hesitated. "Scott really told you to come talk to me?"

"Yes. Does he know you've diagnosed me?"

She shook her head.

"Well, what is it?" he asked, somewhat relieved she'd admitted to being weird around him. Her awkward uncertainty over sharing what she'd ascertained gave her a rather attractive quality.

"I think you have an upside-down parent mindset."

"What does that mean?"

"You feel responsible for your mom and want to fix things and provide for her, even though it's not your job."

He considered this. He couldn't deny he felt that way. But he'd always viewed it as a child's duty to care for their parents when they were older. Even the Bible talked about it. But Heather seemed to think there was something upside down about how he felt. "So, what do I do?" he asked.

"Well, it's not something you just get over in a few minutes or even days. It results from childhood trauma and needs to be worked through, but basically it involves focusing on yourself and what *you* need, rather than focusing on Andi's needs. Set boundaries and stop putting her needs above your own. Learn what it was you missed out on as a child and how it affected you. I can recommend some books if you like, but I can't be your therapist."

A car pulled up next to Mom's car, and they both glanced at it, giving him time to consider her last statement.

"My Thursday group is arriving. You're welcome to stay."

"Thanks. I have some stuff I need to take care of tonight. I would like those book recommendations, though."

"Okay, I can write them down for you right now." She motioned for him to follow her. They went through the door she'd come out of earlier. It was a small office with a worn wooden desk, a vintage-looking swivel chair, and three bookcases along the back wall.

Heather sat in the old chair and grabbed a notebook from the corner of her desk. Ripping a piece of paper out of it, she scribbled on it.

He watched her and thought about her diagnosis of him. They hadn't talked long at the beach, and he didn't know how much she really knew about this upside-down parent thing. He couldn't help but wonder if she'd found fault with him similarly in high school.

She finished writing the list and handed it to him.

He took it, folded it, and put into his back pocket without looking at it. "Thanks."

"You're welcome," she said, getting up from her seat.

"Hey, why can't you be my therapist?"

She cleared her throat and glanced down at her desk. "I'm not licensed." She met his gaze again and smiled.

"Right. One more thing."

She waited.

"Is there any chance you diagnosed me in high school?"

"High school?"

He nodded. "You know, when you turned me down?"

Her cheeks turned pink, and she dropped her gaze for a moment. "No, Phillip. I told you then why I wouldn't go out with you." She moved past him, squeezing his arm as she did and sending electric shocks through him. "Let me know if you want to talk more, or have questions, once you read some of those books."

Chapter 29

"Hi, Mr. Porter, it's Phillip Hawkins," he said, clutching his cell phone to his ear. He brought the paper cup of steaming hot coffee to his lips and took a sip as he stared at the beautiful historic building in front of him.

"Mr. Hawkins. Have you decided about moving forward with the building?"

"Actually, I would love to move forward with it, but I can't afford even a fraction of your asking price. I want to see if you'd be willing to negotiate a deal, but first I need to confess something."

Mr. Porter cleared his throat. "Go on."

Since talking with Heather, he'd realized his deal with Casey didn't actually benefit him at all. He'd convinced himself it would give him experience in a new area of business, but in reality, he would have been giving Casey what she wanted so he could give Mom what he thought she needed. And he would have made himself miserable in the process. But the idea that had been growing in his mind for this place excited him, and he hoped he could convince Grant Porter to give him a chance.

"The spa idea wasn't mine. It was Casey Calloway's. She wanted me to convince you to sell so she could tear the place down and build her luxury spa. I've decided it's not worth my time and energy to partner with Casey, but I've been thinking about what you said to me when you showed me the place. How you would prefer it to be a place that benefits locals. I know there are a lot of small farmers, artists, and crafters in Mylin Valley. I want to start a consignment shop. A place for locals to share their goods."

"Hmm."

Phillip left his spot on the pavement in front of the old building and headed back to the park where he'd left Mom's car and waited for Mr. Porter to respond.

"So you're telling me you were trying to trick me into selling to the Calloway family, but now you want me to consider a different deal—and you want me to believe you're in it all by yourself?"

"Yes, sir." He'd expected Mr. Porter to be angry, but had hoped his admission and new idea would foster some trust.

"You ought to count yourself lucky I didn't find out about this plot before you told me and leave it at that."

"Right. Yes, of course. I'm very sorry, Mr. Porter."

The phone went dead. Well, so much for that. His dream sank into a black hole and he felt stupid for thinking he'd be successful. No. He reminded himself he was capable. After Heather had given him a list of books to read, he'd stopped by the library to see if they carried any of them. They'd had one. After signing up for a library card, he checked it out and had been reading it all weekend. The book described him, and his doubts and fears, to a T. It suggested focusing on positive self-talk to combat the lack of outward encouragement he'd received as a child.

Now the first of two other unpleasant tasks—telling Casey he was out. He opted to inform her through a text message. Setting the coffee cup on top of the car, he put his message together, then hit the send button.

He parked the car near the entrance of Fast Lane Mechanics and climbed out. A man in a dark blue jumpsuit with the name Henry embroidered on the breast pocket came out and greeted him. "What can I do for ya?"

"I'm looking for Jake Hawkins. Is he working today?"

The man eyed him for a moment before responding. "Yes sir, come on in. Did he work on your car there?"

"No. He's my dad." He wondered if the guy was being cagey because they got a lot of complaints.

Henry's face lit up. "Ah, Jake's told me all about you. I'm Henry, the co-owner of the place with your dad." He stuck his grease-stained hand out, and Phillip shook it.

"Nice to meet you, Henry."

"Jake is gonna flip when he sees you here. He was sure you'd never show your face around this place. I can't wait to see his reaction."

Phillip smiled at the man and followed him into the work area. Maybe it wasn't complaints; maybe Henry just knew Jake had a lot of bad people in his past and had his back. The smell of grease and oil hit him as he entered and took him back to high school and the job he'd had as a mechanic for a while. Jake had been released from jail that last time, and had been hired on at the same mechanic shop where Phillip was working. And that's when he'd pursued college.

"Jakey boy. Look who's here," Henry yelled.

Phillip couldn't imagine Jake appreciating the nickname 'Jakey boy' very much. Jake was bent over the engine of a black convertible, but he stood and looked their way at Henry's call. His dad wore a dark blue jumpsuit as well. He didn't seem to have much of a reaction, and Phillip wondered if Henry was disappointed. But looking at the man, he saw his excitement and amusement had not diminished.

Jake wiped his hands on a red shop rag and made his way over. "Phillip," Jake said when he reached them and glanced at Henry, who nodded at Jake, clapped him on the back and walked off. "Everything okay?"

"Yeah. More than, actually. I wanted to let you know Mom saw a doctor, got some medication, and is seeing a therapist."

Jake nodded. "That's great. I'm happy for her."

"I also wanted to tell you I forgive you."

Jake frowned and studied the shop rag in his hands, which he continuously wove through his fingers.

"I'm also okay with it if you and Mom still want to talk."

Jake nodded and cleared his throat, but didn't look up. "I think it's best if I keep my distance."

"A lot of things were said at that intervention, but Mom forgave you first. You shouldn't abandon her now."

Jake looked at him then. "She doesn't need me anymore. She has you and Richard and Denise."

"Yeah, but you can help in ways we can't. You'll be the best encourager when she wants to stop the medication, or when she has a rough day. We don't really understand that piece of this process, but you do."

Jake nodded. "Thank you, son. I better get back to work."

Phillip was disappointed that he hadn't convinced his dad, but maybe it was for the best. At least his dad knew he had forgiven him for the past and the door was open if he ever wanted to catch up. All he could do was try.

Chapter 30

"I'm open, I'm open!" Phillip yelled to the teenage boy who had the soccer ball. The boy kicked the ball toward him, and he stopped it from rolling out of bounds. A group of teenagers from the opposite team rushed toward him and he hurried to move the ball down the field, kicking to another of his teammates as the opposite team tried to surround him.

"Don't let them score!" Scott shouted, running past him.

Phillip jogged toward the goal and watched the teens maneuver the ball to open up a space to score a point, but Scott's team pretty well had them blocked. He was looking for an opening so they could pass the ball back to him, but he didn't get an opportunity before the other team stole the ball and started down the other side of the field.

Scott stopped in the middle of the field and held his hands up in a T. "That's game, guys," he said breathlessly.

Groans and complaints came from all sides, and Scott pointed to the parking lot. "Your parents are here, and we're outta time. But this was fun. We'll definitely do this again."

Teenagers began giving each other high-fives as they walked off the field, gathered their things, and headed off with their parents.

"Thanks for coming, man," Scott said, holding his fist out.

Phillip nodded and tried to bump his friend's fist, but didn't make contact. He laughed and tried again. "I'm tired, but it was fun."

Scott slapped him on the back, then headed toward the sideline, where a parent had called for him.

Phillip found his water bottle, which he'd left with a small towel, and took a long drink before wiping the sweat from his forehead. On the opposite side of the park, Heather was loading four horses into a trailer. A group of people stood nearby, holding rolled-up yoga mats. During the game, he'd caught glimpses of the group, but with his focus on the game he didn't know what was going on.

Curious, he headed that direction. By the time he reached the horse trailer, most of the yoga crowd had dispersed.

"Hey," he said, walking up to Littlefoot, the horse Heather had paired him with when he observed her group therapy. He rubbed the horse's nose.

"Hi, how's it going?" Heather asked, stepping out of the trailer.

"Not bad. Your brother convinced me to come play soccer with the kids he mentors."

"Yeah, I saw you over there."

His stomach twisted. Had she been watching him specifically? "So, did I see what I thought I saw over here?"

She laughed. "Horse yoga?"

He nodded.

"Yes, but I wasn't leading it."

"Ah, so you just provide the horses." Littlefoot snorted and moved his head out of Phillip's reach.

"Yes. Meadow and Arlo Hanlon own a 'yoga with goats' studio a few blocks from here."

"I'm sorry. Did you say, yoga with goats?"

She chuckled. "Yep. They've tried a variety of animals over the years, but so far the only ones to stick are goats and horses."

"Huh. So, did you offer them the horses, or did they reach out to you?" He stepped forward and patted the side of Littlefoot's face.

"They approached me. I've known Meadow and Arlo since I first opened my horse rescue. I hold a fundraising event every year in August, and they always donate a session of yoga with goats for the raffle. When they decided to try horse yoga, they were having trouble finding well-trained horses. Apparently, they thought any horse would do and bought two to practice with. Meadow nearly broke her leg after one horse threw her."

"Yikes." Littlefoot pawed the ground and shook his head. "I don't think this horse likes me."

Heather laughed. "Littlefoot, are you being cantankerous?" The horse nuzzled the pocket of her jeans. "I'm out of carrots, buddy." She scratched his nose, then kissed it. "Littlefoot takes a while to warm up to new people. He was in a traumatic accident five years ago, and it took me almost a year to get him comfortable with me. So don't take it personally."

"But he's so good with that kid."

Heather smiled. "Xavier. Yeah, I know. I'm pretty sure Littlefoot likes Xavier more than anyone."

He nodded and stared at Littlefoot, who eyed him warily.

"So, how are … things?"

"Things?" he asked.

She grinned. "You, your mom?"

"Uh, Mom's doing really well right now. Taking her medication, going to all her appointments. She even started sewing again. An old hobby she used to enjoy."

"That's great. Have you read any of those books I recommended?"

"Yeah. I borrowed one from the library right after I spoke with you. I'm nearly finished with it."

"And?"

"Eye-opening. It's a lot to process."

"Yeah, it can be. But it's not overwhelming, is it? Because you don't want that."

"No. Not overwhelming."

"Good." She fidgeted with the end of her braid. "So, since your mom is doing better, does that mean you'll be leaving again soon?" She broke eye contact and reached for Littlefoot's lead.

"Actually, I've decided to move back." His shoulders tensed as he watched for her reaction.

She looked at him, her brows knit together. "Oh." She turned away and led Littlefoot into the trailer.

He rubbed the back of his neck. That wasn't the reaction he'd hoped for. At her barn, she'd admitted to acting weird after diagnosing him at the lake. But now he was on track to getting his issues resolved. His mom was doing well. Was he just a project to her? He turned toward the open grassy area he'd left and looked for Scott.

"Hey!" Casey's angry voice reached his ears, and he looked in the direction the sound had come from. She marched toward him, her hair pulled into a ponytail that bobbed behind her head. "What the hell were you thinking?" She shoved him but not so hard that he lost his balance. He turned to face her and raised his arms in a defensive position. "How dare you break our agreement and tell Grant Porter I was involved?" She pointed her finger in his face. "I have an extensive network of investors and people in the business world. You will never do business in this town, or in California. I'm going to make sure of it." And she turned and marched away.

He dropped his hands to his sides and blew out a breath.

"So … I see that's going well," Heather said, coming out of the trailer again.

He kept his gaze on Casey's retreating back and sighed. "Yeah."

"You aren't moving because of the whole spa thing, then?"

"No." He replayed Heather's reaction to his news in his mind and turned to face her. "Wait … is that why you …" he pointed at her, then the trailer.

"Yes." A slight blush spread across her cheeks.

He grinned. "Yeah, that's over with."

She nodded. "Good. It was a terrible idea."

He chuckled. "Diagnosing me wasn't the only reason you've been weird, is it?"

"No." She blushed and grabbed the lead for the last horse she needed to load.

Encouraged by this revelation he stepped toward her. "Hey, do you want to have dinner with me on Saturday night?"

The blush deepened, but she met his gaze and smiled. "I would love to."

Chapter 31

Walking up to the Fletcher door, Phillip ran a hand over the front of his dark gray button-up dress shirt and checked the collar before knocking.

A moment later, Heather opened the door and stepped out. "Hi."

"Hello," he said, giving her a once-over. "You look beautiful." Her hair hung loose around her face and she wore a black belted tunic top with daisies on it, black leggings, and brown calf-high boots.

"Thanks, you look nice too."

"Shall we?"

She nodded, and he made his way down the steps in front of her and opened the passenger side door of Mom's car for her. "Why thank you, kind sir," she said as she ducked inside.

He chuckled, closed the door and jogged to the driver's side and climbed in. "Are you still okay with the Italian place I messaged you about yesterday?"

"Yeah, I love that place."

He started the car and drove down the long dirt driveway. "Does your grandpa still live in that other house?"

"No. He died two years ago."

"Oh, I'm sorry."

"It's okay. We knew it was coming. He was getting pretty frail and started needing round-the-clock care. Mom and

Dad hired a nurse to be there when we couldn't, and my brother Parker flew out and stayed with him for a couple of weeks. He even got to meet his great-grandson. We all got to say goodbye, and he passed in his sleep. We miss him, but it was his time. He was almost a hundred years old."

He glanced at her and smiled. "That's definitely an achievement. Are you using the house for your business?"

"I've thought about it, but no. Right now, it's just storage. We had a bunch of stuff in the barn's loft. I moved all that out and into the house because I needed space for more hay."

He nodded. As they headed down the canyon into town, an awkward silence settled between them. Phillip tried to come up with something else to ask her, to keep her talking, but his mind had gone blank. It wasn't a good sign if they'd already run out of things to talk about.

About halfway down, he tried again. "Are you working with any new horses right now?"

"Two."

He waited, but she didn't offer any more. When the road straightened a bit, he glanced over at her. She looked tense and stared out the front window. "Are you okay?"

"Sorry, this road always makes me nervous."

He relaxed a little and smiled. "I have a stellar driving record. You're in safe hands."

She laughed. "I'm sure I am, but you only make up half the equation."

He shrugged. "True. Tell me about the horses," he coaxed gently.

She blew out a breath. "The new horses are two females that were brought to me because the owner couldn't afford to keep them anymore. They're excellent horses, and I won't have to do much with them before I can try to find them new homes."

"You won't try to keep them for your therapy groups?"

"Probably not. I like them, and they would do well as therapy animals, but once I start this master's program I won't have a lot of extra time to train."

He nodded, wondering if she would have time to date once she started school, or if she'd even considered that yet.

The restaurant wasn't too far from the mouth of the canyon. Once they reached the bottom, he sensed Heather relax.

Inside, they waited for their table. The place was crowded and a line of people stood against the entrance wall, waiting to be seated. He was glad he'd called yesterday and made a reservation. Going up to the podium, he gave his name, and a moment later, they were ushered to a small table along the back wall. Classical music played softly in the background, and a small chandelier of fake candles flickered above them.

They sat down, declined any alcohol, and looked over their menus.

"What do you recommend?" he asked, peering at her over the top of his menu.

"Everything." She smiled. "Super helpful, I know, but seriously, everything here is amazing."

A few minutes later, the waitress returned with two glasses of water and a small plate of bread and took their order. Salmon for Heather, fillet medallions for him.

"Now that you're staying in Mylin Valley, what are your plans?" Heather asked.

"Finding a job is the highest priority. Then find a place of my own. I need to fly to California and get all my stuff, and wrap up a few loose ends in a couple of weeks. Beyond that, I'm not positive."

She trailed her index finger around the rim of her water glass. "Does that mean you're giving up on starting your own business?"

"For now. I'd still love to do something with that building on Third Street, but I can't afford it. And I don't think Grant Porter wants to do business with me anymore, anyway."

"Weren't you making apps or something? Do you still want to do that?"

"Maybe, but if Casey Calloway is to be taken seriously, I might have some trouble with that."

Heather picked up her glass and took a sip of the water. "Didn't you date her?" she asked, setting the glass down.

"Briefly, yes. In high school."

"That's right, I remember. You didn't date her because I turned you down, did you?"

Phillip grinned. "No. At least, I don't think so."

"What does that mean?" she laughed.

"Casey came up to me at a party and kissed me. She didn't even know my name, but after that she pretty much dragged me around and ..." He shrugged. "I was her boyfriend for the summer, I guess." He laughed. "It was all a little strange, and I don't know if I went along with it because I'm a guy and she seemed into me, or because you turned me down the week before and I was heartbroken." He gave her a teasing smile.

Heather shook her head and laughed. "I remember Scott telling me about that night. He was jealous of you."

Phillip snorted. "Are you kidding?"

She laughed. "No, he had a huge crush on Casey."

"That's hilarious. He never told me that. By the middle of that summer, I would have insisted on some kind of scheme to get them together, because I was over it."

"If she was so horrible, why did you consider going into business with her?"

"She offered me a way to make up for failing my mom. Or what I thought was a failure."

She tilted her head to the side and looked questioningly at him.

"I never had plans to go to college until I found myself working in the same mechanic shop my dad was working at. He'd gotten out of jail again recently and gotten a job where I worked. I didn't want to be like him in any way, and I knew my best option for getting off that path was to go to school. I also wanted to make sure Mom never had to work two jobs again in her life or worry about how the bills were going to be paid. When Richard called and told me Mom was in the hospital and I came back here, I realized I'd done exactly what my dad had."

"That's why you think you abandoned her?"

He nodded. "I left her on her own. I didn't think it would take me this long to achieve my goal of being able to provide for her. And then Casey offered me an opportunity. I figured if I could help her out, it would give me enough cash to help Mom and some extra to fund whatever my next project would be."

Heather reached her hand out and squeezed his, sending a jolt through his arm. "Your mom is doing all right, though, isn't she? I mean, financially. Other than caring for your grandmother, she isn't working?"

He shook his head and ran his thumb over her fingers. "No, but seeing her so … sad, and unlike herself, convinced me her state of mind was somehow my fault." He smiled at her. "In other words, your diagnosis of me was spot on."

She blushed. "So you can see that these things aren't your fault, then?"

"I think so."

She gave his hand another gentle squeeze. "Good."

Their food arrived, and he reluctantly released her hand.

As they began eating, he started to say something, but stopped.

"What?" Heather asked.

He shook his head self-conscious.

"Come on, tell me," she prodded.

"Are you sure my being an unbeliever was the only reason you turned me down in high school?"

She blushed and wiped her mouth with her napkin, then nodded. "The only reason."

"Not even the fact that Scott and I used to get in so much trouble?"

She laughed. "Not even that. You were my high school crush, Phillip."

He sat back, "Really?"

She nodded. "I didn't expect you to ask me out; we were so different. But I spent a lot of time thinking about what I would do if you ever did. After hearing so many things in the youth group about purity, and biblical dating principles, and being unequally yoked, I was conflicted. But in the end, I decided it was important to me to follow God's plan. But it was really hard to say no to you, and seeing you with Casey that summer was horrible."

"I'm glad you stuck to your convictions." He straightened in his seat. "It always impressed me how you never seemed to cave to peer pressure."

She grinned and shook her head. "I'm pretty sure most people thought I was stuck up."

"I find that very hard to believe."

As dinner progressed, Heather told him about the classes she'd taken so far. What subjects she loved and hated, as well as the teachers. She told him about meeting Xavier and the struggles she'd had figuring out the best way to teach him. She told him about her dreams, and fears about what it would take to accomplish those dreams.

And he told her about his college days, the girl who'd led him to Christ, the church he attended, his roommates and everything he loved and hated about California.

They continued to talk after the plates were cleared and on the drive home as well. Phillip couldn't remember ever feeling this comfortable sharing anything and everything with someone before. When he pulled up in front of her parents' house, he didn't want the evening to end. But she opened her door and climbed out, and he followed her example. They walked slowly up the front porch steps together, then stopped.

"I had a lot of fun tonight," Heather said.

"Me too. We should go on another date."

She grinned. "I agree."

He took a small step toward her. "Yeah?"

She made her own little step toward him, leaving inches of space between them, and his stomach twisted. "Yeah," she whispered.

"Heather?"

"Hmm?"

"I really like you." He stroked her cheek with his thumb. "I always have," he whispered as he leaned in and touched her lips with his.

Her hands rested lightly on his chest, and as the kiss deepened, he wrapped his arms around her waist, but resisted the urge to pull her closer. After a few seconds, they parted. She smiled up at him and he returned it, feeling like the luckiest man alive.

Back home, Phillip sat in the car, replaying the evening over in his head. He wasn't ready to go inside yet to be quizzed by Mom. After a few minutes, he climbed out of the car and headed to the front door, but lingered on the stairs, the chill of the evening spring air felt good on his skin. The entire evening felt like a dream and he wondered, not for the first time that night, if Heather genuinely liked him as much as she seemed to on their date. It didn't seem possible, after all these years, that he would get the girl who had seemed so far out of his reach.

"Phillip?"

A voice on the sidewalk startled him out of his reverie. "Mrs. Eberly. What are you doing out here so late?"

She waved a hand at him. "I'm old. I don't sleep much. I saw you pass by and wanted to speak with you."

He wondered if she sat at her front window and watched everyone all day and night. "Okay, what about?" He tensed, wondering if he'd gotten himself in trouble with the old woman somehow.

"How was your date with Miss Fletcher this evening?"

He furrowed his brow. "How did you know about that?"

She smiled. "A young man visiting his mother because of a medical crisis rarely packs brand new slacks and dress shirts."

He looked down at himself, wondering if he'd missed removing some creases.

"I noticed you've been wearing the same few outfits since your arrival," she offered.

"You figured out I was taking Heather on a date because of the clothes I'm wearing?"

She laughed. "Of course not. But I saw the two of you at church, and around town."

"It was that obvious I liked her?"

"Oh, dear boy, a blind man could see your interest in one another from a mile away."

He chuckled and stuck his hands in his pockets, wondering what she'd observed, and feeling pleased that Heather's interest in him had been just as obvious to Mrs. Eberly. He certainly hadn't figured out how Heather felt about him until yesterday. Mrs Eberly really did know everything. If she was ever to tell him she could read minds, he would absolutely believe it.

"So, how was the date?"

"Uh, great."

She smiled. "I'm glad to hear it. That's not why I came over here, though."

"Oh?"

"I heard about your dealings with Miss Calloway and that old building on Third Street."

"What? How?" What other surprises could she throw at him?

She cleared her throat. "Because I'm the actual owner of that building, not Mr. Porter."

He ran a hand over his face. "What?"

"Miss Calloway isn't the only shrewd businesswoman in this little town. I hired Mr. Porter to act as manager for me. He makes sure the building stays in good shape, and agreed to tell anyone who asked that he was the owner. But he reported any interest in the place to me."

"I don't understand. Why?"

She tapped her index finger against her forehead. "The Calloways have wanted that piece of property for years now. And I always refused to sell it to them. They wouldn't have appreciated the historical value, the legacy of it. My husband's family built that bank and were the first bankers in this town. When the bank closed, he didn't want to give the building up, and we didn't have to. It was paid for; we only had to pay taxes on it. So why not keep it? When he died, he left the place to me in his will. It was his wish that the bank remain standing, and if it had to be sold, that it be sold to someone who would respect the building and its history. The Calloway family were not those people."

"Why are you telling me this?"

"Because I think you've turned out to be a good, honest, hard-working young man. Mr. Porter told me of your alternative plan. The consignment shop. I think it's a lovely idea."

"Thank you, but I wasn't upfront with Mr. Porter. I didn't tell him about Casey's involvement."

"I'm aware. But in the end, you did the right thing. I know you can't afford the price tag I told Mr. Porter to give you. But I like your plan, and I want to give you a chance to make it a reality. I would like to discuss some possibilities with you next week, if you're open to it."

"Really? I mean, yes. That sounds great. I would love that."

She smiled and held out her hand. "Very good."

He shook her hand.

"Monday good for you?" she asked.

"Yes, absolutely. Thank you, Mrs. Eberly."

"Of course. Every young man who's beginning their journey to love and family should get a strong start to their career if they can." She winked at him and sauntered off down the street.

He stared after her in disbelief, then shook his head and went into the house.

Chapter 32: Epilogue

"Are you ready?" Heather asked, poking her head into the upstairs office of Hawkins Consignment.

He stood up from the desk and nodded. "Do I look okay?"

She stepped into the room and gave him a once-over. "More than okay."

He grinned at her.

"You look very handsome and professional, and a little nervous," she said, stepping up to him and kissing his cheek.

He wrapped his arm around her and kissed her. "Then you better stay close. I'm less nervous with you around."

"Don't worry, I'm not going anywhere."

A knock came from the doorway. "There's a crowd gathering outside. Are you ready?" Mom asked.

"Yeah."

They left the office, and Phillip closed the door behind him. He glanced around at the shelves full of beautifully hand-crafted ceramic and wooden dishes that filled one section of the loft, the shelf of books written by local authors in another, and jewelry in the center.

Downstairs, toward the front of the building, was a section of fresh produce, honey, eggs, and milk from local farmers. Clothing and blankets, including Mom's latest creations, hung on racks in the middle, and handmade toys lined the shelves along the wall behind the stairs. He'd packed the store with amazing creations from people and local businesses in the valley, and today was opening day. Richard and Denise straightened up the clothing racks as he, Heather, and Mom came downstairs. Scott stood behind the counter showing a teenager how to use the cash register.

It had taken him four months to convince people to sell their wares in his shop while he set up the store and got the building restored. And with Mrs. Eberly's help, he'd found wallpaper that nearly matched the original. She'd agreed to hire a contractor with knowledge of historic buildings and they'd restored all the wood, which now gleamed like new.

They'd agreed on a price for the building. Far below that which she'd offered to him when he was working with Casey. He would make the payment to her every month, with no interest. If she died before he could finish paying it off, she'd created an agreement that stated his monthly payment would go to the Catholic church food bank until the sum they agreed on was reached.

When he asked her why the Catholic church and not his uncle's church, she'd said it would be a conflict of interest for him and because she didn't trust Richard not to use it for some cockamamie idea of his. Families still needed food, and this way she'd be sure the money was helping people in the way she intended.

"Where's Mrs. Eberly?" he asked, looking around and not seeing her.

"I think she was putting bouquets of flowers in the bathrooms," Denise said, with an amused grin.

"Yes, I was, and now everything looks absolutely perfect." She came into the main store area and smiled at him. "Ready to get this show on the road? We don't want to keep these people waiting forever."

"I'm ready." He held out his hand to Mrs. Eberly, but she waved it away.

"This is your store and yours only. You invite them in."

He opened the doors and stepped out into the unusually warm autumn morning. They'd put rope across the entrance so he could make his welcome speech before everyone rushed in. Everyone clapped, and he waited for the noise to die down.

"Thank you for coming to the grand opening of Hawkins Consignment!"

More cheers.

"I'm so thankful to all the talented individuals who put their trust in me through this process. I can't wait for you to see all the amazing things they've made and put their hearts and souls into. As I've met with our artists and farmers and gotten to know them, I've heard the stories behind what they make, and I'm honored to showcase these amazing gifts with all who live here and who will come and visit our valley.

"Thank you for coming to celebrate the grand opening with us. Many of the people who created the items and the small farmers who grew and raised the food in our store will be here throughout the day, so please, search them out, ask them about what they do, and let's support our local friends and families!"

He took the rope down but stayed by the door, greeting people, shaking hands and making sure the line kept moving at a good pace.

"This is really amazing, son."

Phillip paused and glanced over his shoulder. Jake stood off to the side, behind him. "Thanks." He hadn't heard from Jake since the day he went to see him at the mechanic's shop. Mom hadn't either. "Are you coming in?"

"You sure?" he twirled an unlit cigarette between his fingers.

"Yes, of course I am." He stepped back and made room for his dad to squeeze through and held his hand out for a shake.

Jake nodded, stuck the cigarette back in his pocket, shook the offered hand, and passed through.

Once most of the crowd had entered, Phillip allowed himself to look at the packed store. He'd done it. He'd actually done it.

Harry Fletcher senior approached him and shook his hand. "Good work here, Mr. Hawkins. We're all mighty proud of you."

"Thank you, sir."

"Are you still planning on joining us for dinner tomorrow evening?"

"Yes, sir." A month after he had moved into his own apartment in the valley and a month and a half after he and Heather started dating, Harry had showed up at his place to have a "heart-to-heart," as he called it. After a terrifying, one-sided, twenty-minute conversation in which Harry made it clear there would be consequences if Phillip broke his daughter's heart, he invited him to the Fletcher family dinner that took place once a month. He didn't refuse. Heather insisted her father was all bark and no bite, but he didn't want to risk ever getting on the man's bad side.

"Amy and I are probably going to head out soon, but we'll be back when it's a little less crazy in here," Harry said.

"Sounds good."

He nodded and disappeared into the crowd again. Phillip wasn't sure if it was because Harry had put the fear of God into him, or simply the fact that Heather's family seemed to accept him, but it meant a lot to know Harry was proud of the work he'd done.

Phillip saw Mom, Grandma, and Heather near the rack, holding the clothes Mom had made. He headed their direction, slipping his arm around Heather's waist.

"Hi, Grandma. What do you think of all this?" he asked.

"Oh, it's a busy day at the market. I like to shop when it's less busy. Have you seen these?" She fingered a shirt on the rack.

"I have." He smiled at Mom.

"I've never heard of this brand, PB Clothing, before. Is it a new design company?"

"Uh, kind of. A local woman makes these from her house."

Grandma's eyes widened. "They're so professional. I never would have thought someone could have done this from their house. Do you know who the seamstress is? I'd like to congratulate them."

"I do. You're standing right next to her."

Grandma looked surprised, but looked at Heather instead of Mom.

"Other side, Grandma."

"What?"

"Mom made these." He pointed at her.

Grandma looked at Andi, and Phillip hoped she was having a lucid moment so Mom could tell her how she'd named her clothing brand after her. The PB stood for Phyllis Barker.

"Oh my dear, you are very talented. I haven't seen sewing like this in a long time. Your mother should be very proud."

"Thanks. She is," Andi said.

"What time is it?" Grandma asked.

"Nine in the morning," Andi said.

"I need to be back for my recital by noon."

"I know, Mom. We'll have you there, I promise," Andi said.

They had moved Grandma into a nursing home about Three months ago, and she had transitioned remarkably well. During her second week there, she sat down at a piano and played for the first time in years. The facility had a day each week set aside for residents to showcase their talents. In every other aspect of her life, her memory continued to fade, but when it came to her weekly music recital, she had yet to forget about it.

Jake lingered nearby, glancing in their direction every so often. Phillip nudged Mom and pointed him out.

"Let's go talk to him," Mom said.

"I'll stay with Phyllis," Heather said.

Phillip smiled at her and went with his mother.

"Jake, you came," Andi said, giving him a hug.

He nodded.

"I'm glad. I've been meaning to call you. To thank you for the intervention. I saw my doctor and started seeing a therapist."

Jake nodded again. "Phil told me. That's good."

"Wait, you haven't talked with each other since we were all at the house?" Phillip asked.

Jake and Andi both shook their heads.

"Then how did you know about this?" Phillip asked.

"Saw it advertised in the paper. Figured a shop with my last name on it, up here in the valley, could only be your doing," Jake said.

Phillip smiled. "I'm glad you came, Dad."

Jake nodded.

"I hope we can still talk now and then," Andi said.

Jake wiped a hand across his nose and looked around the room, then shrugged. "I should probably go."

"Are you sure?" Andi asked.

Jake nodded.

"Thanks for stopping by, Dad." Phillip stuck his hand out and Jake gripped it firmly.

"I'm proud of you, kid."

After four months of taking medication and going to therapy, Mom was doing better. She still had rough days, but they were manageable. And while she still felt able to care for Grandma, she'd decided it was time for her to focus on her own health. Sewing helped. She even started offering sewing classes to a couple of kids on the weekends and found she loved it.

He scanned the room. Several people waved or nodded at him and congratulated him as they walked past. Heather stood across the room, chatting with her friend Cleo. She'd started her master's program two months ago. He had worried they would grow apart before they even really got to know each other. Especially since she also had to plan her fundraiser for the year at the same time. But she had roped him into helping and, even though he'd been insanely busy getting this place ready to go, they'd agreed to set aside one night a week as a date night. She made it clear he was as important to her as she was to him.

Four months ago, he was convinced he didn't belong here; had never belonged in Mylin Valley. Now he was back with his family and had more friends and acquaintances than he could ever have fathomed. And for the first time, he felt like he was finally home.

The End

A Note from the Author

I started writing this book in 2019. It was originally supposed to be the first book in the Mylin Valley series, but as I wrote it, another story came to life in my mind. One I felt needed to be told first. Not because the story itself was more important, but because I needed to learn and understand some things before I could make this story everything it was supposed to be.

So, Finding Purpose became book 1 in the series. After I finished Finding Purpose and again sat down to write Finding Home I was afraid I still wouldn't be ready to write it. However, I was pleasantly surprised to find that the writing came fast and easy.

This book, while containing all the original characters I'd come up with, looks nothing like I thought it would when I first came up with the idea. I had originally intended Phillip for the church. He was going to be a pastor, and his uncle's replacement. And while all the other elements of the story worked the way I wanted them to, this one factor bothered me no end and I couldn't figure out why.

As I wrote Heather's story, I realized I didn't necessarily want another pastor to take over Mylin Valley Life Church. I wanted to see what would happen if members of the church were equipped to grow in real, honest, authentic relationships with each other.

Angela E. Powell

During the writing of Finding Purpose, I was studying the book of Acts in my daily Bible reading. I was specifically looking to see what church leadership looked like at that time. And what I found was a hierarchy of believers who came together as often as they could to search out the scriptures and pray together.

This hierarchy was made up of the eleven disciples who were closest to Jesus, other believers who had seen, heard, and followed Jesus, believers who witnessed his death and possibly saw him after he was resurrected or came to believe in his resurrection from the witness of the other believers, and new believers who heard the disciples preaching and accepted God's free gift, but hadn't necessarily heard Jesus for themselves.

There were no church buildings, no start time, no end time, no expectations as far as how long worship lasted, or how long the preaching went on. And yet these people also had jobs to go to, families to care for, etc. I started asking myself what would that look like in our world today? Where would Christians meet if there were no more church buildings? How would we organize ourselves? What would we do the same? What would we do differently? What values do we hold in church that would not convert to this other way of living for Jesus? How many people would put in the effort to gather with other believers without a set time or place to fit it into our schedules? How many wouldn't put in the effort?

With these questions in mind, along with the dwindling numbers of younger people I see and hear about in church these days, I tried to see things from the perspective of a pastor and it seemed a scary thing to be facing a world where pastors were phased out, and no longer needed as they are today.

In book 1 Richard Barker is faced with these questions but to a lesser degree. As a result, he introduces a new way of doing church after discovering new scientific evidence showing how we were created to be relational people. Richard is a background character in book 1 so you don't see much of his journey there. Now, four years later he's struggling. He believes he's failed in what God wanted him to do as a pastor because he expected better results from the changes he made. He's also tired of the daily grind, the constant bombardment on his time and mental capacity from the members of his church.

It's through his struggle that he begins to question the legacy of his church. What will become of it? Who will be the next pastor? What happens if there is no next pastor?

I purposefully left the conclusion to his questions out of the book because I honestly don't know the answer. I'm not sure anyone does. And I'm not sure we're even close to being in a place where the majority of Christians are thinking about this either, despite the large number of believers I've heard talking about how they long for something different and more authentic. But I am curious, what IF church in America stopped being church as we know it? How do YOU think it would look?

Another reason I decided I didn't want Phillip to be a young pastor is because most Christians don't think about becoming a pastor these days. I wanted Phillip to be an everyday guy. A young man who loves the Lord, seeks the Lord, isn't totally satisfied with how he sees the church operating, but has no idea how to fix it and doesn't really see the responsibility of fixing it as something that falls on his shoulders.

Besides, the more I got to know Phillip, the less he seemed fit for the role of a pastor. He doesn't like drawing too much attention to himself, prefers to keep his private life private, and the more we got to know each other, the more he made it clear he didn't want to deal with his family drama while trying to figure out how to be a pastor at the same time. In short, I felt he had too many areas he needed to grow in to fit the idea of a pastor that could take over for Richard.

Also, I can't see Heather being a pastor's wife with everything she has going on. Of course, I could be getting ahead of myself and maybe I shouldn't hint at wedding bells just yet. We'll have to see what book 3 throws their way.

In keeping with the theme of invisible disabilities, depression made an appearance in this book. Depression may be better understood than Fetal Alcohol Spectrum Disorder in today's world, but it's still easy to hide and still has the stigma of shame attached to it.

I chose this disability because I know people who have struggled with depression and went through a period of it myself as a young adult. I know what it feels like to want to stay in bed and hide for days on end. And I know what it feels like to want to hide those sad, discouraging, intrusive thoughts from your loved ones.

Andi's depression stems from relational trauma. Both from her abusive marriage to Jake, and from her religious, overbearing parents. I wanted to show how relational trauma can cause us to see God in a jaded light. Andi doesn't come to Jesus in the book, but as you learn, she does know about Him. But the people in her life leave her with a bad taste in her mouth for the things of God.

There are a lot of juxtaposing themes in this book. The different ways Andi and Richard deal with their childhood religious experience is just one of them. I felt it was important to show more than one side, to make it clear that no one person will respond to a situation the same as another. We're all different and we need to remember that when our lives intersect with the lives of others. Because when it comes to sharing Jesus, the way we present Him can be a light, or a light snuffer. Without a deeper, relational understanding of who stands before us, we may not send the message of light we think we're sending.

There are some deep, somewhat dark themes in this book, but I hope in the end it brings you encouragement, makes you think, and is intriguing enough to keep you turning the pages into the wee hours of the morning.

Blessings,

Angela E. Powell

Acknowledgments

I thank God for giving me the idea for this series and for waking me up one morning to point out a few places where what I wrote sounded rather judgmental of my fellow Christians, which is never my intention. I am grateful that I serve a God who cares about all the little things that feel like big things to me and is willing to talk to me about them.

Big thanks go to my mom who let me talk her ear off about this book while trying to remain vague about the main plot points so as not to spoil it for her. Most of the time she had no idea what or who I was talking about, but she listened happily and patiently.

As always, thanks to my husband, Craig, for supporting my dreams as an author, farmer, businesswoman, rooster whisperer, and animal lover. My dreams might not make us much money at the present, but you support me anyway.

Thank you to my editor, Doreen Martens. And thanks to 100Covers for the amazing job they did on the cover design.

And of course, I can't forget you, dear readers. Thank you for supporting my work. Your purchase of my books, your reviews, and your notes of encouragement mean the world to me.